REA

Fiction
Peel, Colin D.
Dark armada

✓

DARK ARMADA

By the same author

Adapted to Stress
Bitter Autumn
One Sword Less
On a Still Night
Cold Route to Freedom
Flameout
Nightdive
Hell Seed
Glimpse of Forever
Snowtrap
Firestorm
Hell's Arena
Atoll
Covenant of the Poppies

Writing as Lindsey Grey

Smoke From Another Fire

Colin D. Peel

DARK
ARMADA

St. Martin's Press ❧ New York

DARK ARMADA. Copyright © 1995 by Colin D. Peel.
All rights reserved. Printed in the United States of
America. No part of this book may be used or
reproduced in any manner whatsoever without
written permission except in the case of brief
quotations embodied in critical articles or reviews.
For information, address St. Martin's Press,
175 Fifth Avenue, New York, N.Y. 10010.

Library of Congress Cataloging-in-Publication Data

Peel, Colin D.
Dark armada / by Colin D. Peel.
p. cm.
"A Thomas Dunne Book."
ISBN 0-312-13460-6 (hardcover)
1. Explosions—South Pacific Ocean—Fiction.
2. Weapons systems—Testing—Fiction.
3. Engineers—United States—Fiction.   I. Title.
PR6066.E36D37   1995
823'.914—dc20   95-34520   CIP

First published in Great Britain by
Robert Hale Limited

First U.S. Edition: December 1995
10 9 8 7 6 5 4 3 2 1

I am Alpha and Omega, the beginning and the ending, saith the Lord, which is, and which was and which is to come, the Almighty.

Revelation 1. v.8

This book is for
Weathertop Sparrowhawk

Prologue

Barely visible, supported by warm air drifting upwards from the sea, the dust was thinning. It was spread out now, a stratified layer of tiny particles suspended high above the Pacific to form a sheet that was already more than half a mile cross.

Below it the sea was still. From Cape Alexander on Choiseul to the eastern tip of San Cristobal 500 miles away, the ocean surrounding the Solomon Islands was as flat and grey as the sky had been for the last three days, and with neither a breeze nor air currents to disperse the dust, the particles hung like weightless specks of matter trapped between the heavens and the sea.

Viewed at a distance from the cockpit of his aircraft, to Warren Decker the dust first appeared to be nothing more than a solitary wisp of cloud, an almost transparent area of haze or mist which somehow had become detached from the ceiling of higher and more solid cloud. It was indistinct, so much so that on the two occasions he looked away and then tried to find it again, he could not be sure it was still there.

But it was still there, Decker decided. He hadn't imagined it, and now he was closer, the mist or the vapour was easier to pick out. He could also see that it formed a layer, an ill-defined and somewhat blurry layer, but a layer nonetheless – something that in fifteen years of flying, Decker could not recall having seen before.

He became more interested, banking the aircraft so he could examine the mist from the west with the light behind him.

But what light there was filtering through the cloud made little difference, and it was not until Decker realized he was looking at the layer edge-on that the need for him to increase altitude became more obvious.

For a moment he almost decided not to bother. He was already off course, and without wasting time out here in the middle of nowhere for no good reason, it would still be late afternoon before he reached the airstrip on Malaita.

Not that it mattered much, Decker thought. Economizing on fuel wouldn't make the trip from Kira Kira pay for itself, and unless he could pick up a passenger at Auki, the whole damn flight was going to be a waste of time anyway.

Ahead of him, a single ray of sunlight had found its way through the cloud cover. It was slanting down to illuminate the mist, a slender finger of light in an otherwise drab and empty sky. And where it touched the mist – where it passed through whatever the mist was made of – Decker could see more layers: dark bands, lighter bands and parts where the light was made to sparkle from countless millions of reflections.

He pulled back on the stick, no longer merely interested but intrigued and curious to discover what the phenomenon could be.

The Airtech Eagle climbed steadily until at 8,000 feet Decker abandoned the manoeuvre.

Long before he had levelled out, the ray of sunlight had vanished and with it had gone the strange banding and the sparkle.

Now, although he could see the full extent of the layer,

there was nothing interesting about it, nothing to have justified his curiosity and, to Decker's disappointment, the mist seemed if anything to be more transparent than it had been before.

He checked his instruments before resetting his course for Auki, then let the Eagle slowly lose altitude until the aircraft entered the edge of the mist itself.

Decker realized his mistake at once.

The mist was dust – fine, atmospheric dust, sparsely distributed but enough of it to be ingested by the engine and enough for him to see it swirling over the wings and all around the cockpit canopy.

Increasing his angle of descent, Decker swore out loud. In such small quantities the dust was unlikely to harm the engine, but it was stupid of him to have taken the risk when there had been no need, especially on an unscheduled flight this far out from the islands.

He was almost clear of the dust when the first signs of trouble started to appear.

Sparks were streaming from the Eagle's exhaust, red sparks trailing back over the fuselage as though a firework had gone off inside the engine cowling. They were followed by bursts of more brilliant, whiter sparks.

Decker grabbed at the throttle, and was leaning forwards to punch the button on his radio when the sky exploded.

In less than a tenth of a second, combustion waves and a flame-front travelling at the speed of sound, turned the dust cloud into a fireball of burning gas so violent and of such proportions that the movement of the surrounding air was too slow to relieve the pressure.

High above the sea, nearly two square miles of sky had become a boiling mass of incandescent flame. And with the flame came the shock wave and the sound of detonation.

Across the empty reaches of the Pacific a thunderous, rolling roar travelled outwards from the fireball. It lasted for several seconds then, suddenly, as quickly as it had begun, the noise was gone.

A pall of smoke stretched upwards now, spiralling out of a giant hole in the cloud cover to mix with a column of sunlight that was pouring through to turn the sea from grey to azure blue

Soon even the smoke had disappeared and, where a few minutes ago the blast had disturbed the ocean surface, all that remained were ripples and fragments of floating wreckage from the Airtech Eagle.

For the pilot of the Eagle, the end had been mercifully swift. He had died in an instant, unseen and alone, incinerated by an explosion which had taken place in a region of the world so distant that only sea birds and the summer wind would ever know what once had happened here.

One

Jolted awake for the second time in ten minutes, Redman gave up his attempt to sleep. The plane was still lurching about, and on the other side of the aisle, an overhead locker had burst open, spilling its contents of bottles and coats on to one of the seats.

He watched the Air Niugini hostess clear up the mess. The entire flight from Papua New Guinea had been like this, one damn patch of bumpy air after another. It was the islands, he thought. No sooner had the plane flown through hot air rising from a valley than it was out over the sea again.

Taking a map from his seat pocket, he studied it for a moment then looked out the window. The view was much the same as it had been before he'd fallen asleep – a mass of tiny green atolls scattered among the larger islands. The islands, though, were closer now. He could see how mountainous they were and how the rain forests were laced with rivers and ravines.

By turning the map on its side he thought he could identify a group of islands almost immediately below.

The hostess came to help. She leaned across in front of him to see what he was looking at.

'Those are the Russells,' she said. 'Down there to the left.'

'How do you know?'

'We fly in here three times a week.' She smiled. 'First trip to the Solomons?'

Redman nodded.

She pulled back from the window, sitting down in the empty seat beside him.

'How much longer?' he asked. 'To Honiara, I mean.'

'We're just about there.' She glanced at her watch. 'Fifteen minutes. Can I get you anything?'

'No, no thank you.' He put the map back into the seat pocket. 'Are there taxis at the airport, or do I go by canoe?'

She smiled again. 'As long as you're only travelling into town you'll be all right. Honiara's reasonably civilized. There are taxis and minibuses. Where are you staying?'

'The Mendana. Is it OK?'

'It's air-conditioned – that's the main thing out here.' She stood up. 'I'd better go. Have a nice visit.'

'Thanks.' Redman wasn't expecting to have a nice visit. In this part of the world, at this time of year, it was a straight fight with the temperature. It had been hot enough when he'd left Australia but he guessed it would be a lot worse in Honiara than it had been in Brisbane. Even if it wasn't, the trip was still almost certainly a waste of time, he thought, a pointless exercise to satisfy someone in head office on the other side of the Pacific.

The ill-humour stayed with him over the next half-hour, and by the time he had cleared customs and immigration, Redman was beginning to wish he was somewhere else altogether.

Outside the terminal, the heat hit him like a wall. The handle of his case was already sticky in his hand and he could feel sweat running down inside his shirt.

Two buses and three taxis were waiting at the kerb. Only one taxi had its engine running – a sure sign of air-conditioning, Redman decided. He headed for it directly, colliding with a woman who seemed to have the same idea.

'Hey, I'm sorry.' He steadied her by the arm. 'You take this one.'

She was a slightly built European in her late twenties with short brown hair and too much make-up.

'The taxi?' she said.

'Sure.' He released her arm. 'Go ahead. I can get one of these others.'

She gave him a quick artificial smile. 'Are you Steven Redman?'

'That's me.' He was surprised.

'I'm Jennifer Decker. I'm sorry I nearly knocked you over. I wanted to introduce myself before you disappeared in the taxi.'

'Oh.' Redman wasn't sure what to say.

'You know who I am, don't you?'

'Yes.' He hesitated. 'I wasn't expecting you to meet me, though. How did you know I was coming?'

'Mr Hawthorne told me – well, more or less. I telephoned him in California yesterday. He said I should contact your Brisbane office – so I did. They gave me your flight number.'

'Look,' Redman said, 'I don't want to be rude but I'm pretty tired and I could use a shower. I don't think this is a good time or a good place for us to talk, do you?'

'I haven't come to talk to you now. I just thought it would be nice if I met you at the airport and took you to your hotel.' There was the same quick smile. 'In case you didn't know anyone.' She pointed. 'My car's over there.'

Redman accompanied her to a white Nissan.

'You're staying in town, aren't you? That's what your secretary said.' She took his case from him and put it on the rear seat.

'At the Mendana.' He climbed into the car beside her. 'The girl on the plane said it was OK.'

'It's a very good hotel.' She started to pull away from

the kerb but braked before the car had travelled more than a few feet. 'I had to telephone California because I've found out something else,' she said.

Redman was feeling uncomfortable.

'Hold on a second,' he said, 'there's something you'd better understand. I'm not some hot-shot inspector of air accidents. I only run the Australia office for Airtech in Brisbane. Two days ago I got a fax from Hawthorne telling me to get out here and what I'm supposed to do. I'm real sorry about your husband, but I haven't come specifically to talk to you. I'm here because head office think it's a good idea to have someone write an in-house report from the Solomon Islands.'

'I see.' She began driving again. 'Does that mean the report is more important than finding out how my husband died?'

'I didn't say that.'

'Who else are you going to talk to?'

'I don't know yet. I've only been here five minutes.' He kept his eyes on the road.

'This is the Solomons, Mr Redman. I've lived here for over three years. If you think you can find out anything by yourself, you're wrong. Your report's going to be a whole lot of blank sheets of paper.'

'Maybe.' He glanced at her, wondering why she had chosen to turn the disappearance of her husband's plane into a personal crusade against Airtech, and how much trouble she was prepared to make for the company.

The journey into Honiara took less than fifteen minutes. For most of it, Jennifer Decker remained silent. After promising herself not to rush things, as usual she found it impossible to contain her impatience. Now, aware that she had created a bad impression, she was anxious not to worsen matters.

There were fewer people about in town than Redman had anticipated. Unlike Papeete, Suva and most of the other Pacific island centres he'd visited, Honiara had a quiet, almost utilitarian atmosphere. It was the lack of tourists, he thought, or maybe the predominance of dark-skinned people on the streets. Even now, travelling along what was obviously the main road on the waterfront, he had trouble picking out a European.

He was still trying to find one when the Nissan turned into a cul-de-sac and drew up outside the hotel.

'Thanks for the ride,' he said.

'I'm sorry if it sounded as though I was trying to push.' She opened one of the rear doors so Redman could collect his suitcase. 'It's because I've been building up my expectations – you know – because I hoped you'd be able to help. No one else wants to.'

The pathos was pretty thin, Redman thought. But she appeared to be entirely rational. Not at all like the woman Hawthorne had described in his fax. It was even conceivable that she did have something worthwhile to say about her husband's plane crash.

'Look,' he said, 'I'm on a fairly tight schedule, so if you want to talk, what about having dinner with me here tonight?'

'It's nice of you to ask me.' She paused. 'But there's something I have to show you. It'd be a bit difficult to bring with me.'

'Couldn't I see it another time?'

'I suppose so.' She was embarrassed. 'I know you've only just arrived, and I know you're not a hot-shot inspector of air accidents because you've told me you're not, but I'm sure you'll be interested in what I want to tell you. I was hoping you'd have dinner with me at my home. I don't live very far away.'

'OK.' Redman couldn't bring himself to argue. 'Where do I go?'

'I'll write it down for you.' She took a piece of paper from her handbag and scribbled down an address. 'Is seven o'clock too early?'

'No, that's fine.' He read the address. 'I'll see you this

evening, then.'

'Oh, I nearly forgot.' She handed him a package of tablets. 'If you left Australia at short notice you'd better take some of these straight away.'

'What are they?'

'Chloroquine – for malaria. It's a problem here.'

'Well, thank you,' he said. 'Is there anything else I ought to know?'

'Yes, I think so, Mr Redman. I'll tell you about it this evening.' She restarted the car. 'Goodbye.'

After she'd gone, he checked in at reception where he cashed some travellers cheques and arranged for his passport and airline ticket to be kept in a hotel safe deposit box. Then he went directly to his room and spent the next half an hour in the shower. When he emerged he was ready to make his call to California.

The Airtech telephonist recognized his voice.

'Good morning, Mr Redman,' she said. 'Where are you calling from?'

'Honiara and it's afternoon here. Is Mr Hawthorne in yet?'

'Yes, he is. I'll put you through.'

'Hi, Steve.' Hawthorne sounded wary. 'How was the trip?'

'Lousy. Guess who met me at the airport.'

'Don't tell me. Not the Decker woman?'

'Right. She says she phoned yesterday with some new information. I thought I'd check with you before I talk to her properly. What was it about?'

'I don't know. I said she could tell you when you arrived.'

'Thanks.' Redman made no attempt to disguise his irritation. 'That's a lot of help.'

'Hey, Steve, if you're pissed off before you start you might as well catch another plane back to Australia. What's the matter with you?'

'Nothing. I just don't think I can do much good here,

that's all.'

'Talk to some people; find out where Decker had his maintenance work done; see where he bought his fuel.' Hawthorne paused. 'And tell his wife she's not going to get anywhere trying to make out there was something wrong with the aircraft. The stupid bitch has been faxing Australian newspapers. I've had one of them on the phone already.'

'OK.' Redman thought the assignment sounded more like damage control than a technical investigation.

'How long do you figure it's going to take?' Hawthorne asked. 'I don't want this to get in the way of the Indonesian order.'

'I'll call you. A couple of days should fix things here.'

'Right. Have a sniff around while you're there – see what the market's like for light aircraft – we haven't thought of the Solomons before. You never know what you might turn up.'

Instead of pointing out that this hardly seemed the best time to be promoting Airtech Eagles in the Solomon Islands, Redman said goodbye and hung up before Hawthorne could think of any other good ideas.

A parting of the ways was overdue, Redman decided. A couple of years in Australia and three before that in San Francisco were enough. Airtech might have prospered since Hawthorne had taken over as vice president, but the company's attitude had changed a lot. The business had become too big, too impersonal, or just plain arrogant.

Knowing the danger of examining the reason for his own change of attitude, Redman put on a clean shirt and a pair of shorts then headed out to explore downtown Honiara.

Outside it was still unbearably hot. Even close to the water the temperature was much higher than it ever was on the hottest of days in Brisbane and, within a matter of minutes, he found himself seeking out the shade from larger buildings and from the poincianas and palms which lined the street.

He walked east, staying on Mendana Avenue until he reached the harbour. It was crammed with fishing boats, coastal freighters and launches. Here and there, even the odd canoe was tied up at the wharf.

The flavour of the place was of another time, Redman thought, still unspoiled – a working South-Sea town that had yet to be discovered by the rest of the world. The islanders, too, appeared to be unspoiled; happy, friendly people judging by the nods and smiles he was receiving from a group of them coming off one of the boats.

Solomon Islanders were the blackest people Redman had ever seen, some of them startlingly so because of their blond or red hair. He grinned at a large lady who said something to him in pidgin on her way past. She was carrying a fish in one hand, a basket of mangoes in the other.

Despite the heat and Jennifer Decker's warning about malaria, Redman already knew he liked it here. It was a place that offered something he'd encountered only once or twice before on other Pacific islands, a better way of life than sitting in a high-rise office somewhere in Brisbane or San Francisco. Or was it? he wondered. Was it just so different you couldn't decide unless you tried it?

He remained at the waterfront for another fifteen minutes before carrying on towards the Chinese end of town, then retraced his steps to the Point Cruz intersection where he set off to examine the other end of Honiara.

It was past 5.00 when he returned to his hotel, and nearly 6.30 by the time he had showered again and was ready to leave for his dinner engagement. By then, although in better spirits than he had been earlier, Redman was having second thoughts about the wisdom of spending an evening with Jennifer Decker.

The reservations had still not gone away when his taxi drew up outside her house.

She greeted him at the gate while he was paying the driver. 'Good evening, Mr Redman.'

'Hi.' He smiled politely.

Since meeting him at the airport she'd changed into a white blouse and a knee-length cotton skirt pulled in at the waist by a bright red belt. Her make-up was less pronounced than it had been earlier but he could see there was still plenty of it.

He walked beside her across the lawn, considering how he would respond if she began suggesting that the Eagle was an unsafe and unreliable aircraft before they reached the front door. He need not have worried. Determined to rectify the bad impression she had created this afternoon, Jennifer Decker had no intention of making the same mistake again. For the hour before dinner, during the meal and for the entire time Redman was drinking his after-dinner coffee, she successfully kept the conversation away from anything to do with her husband's disappearance.

When the subject was eventually broached, it was Redman who made the opening remark. 'I called Hawthorne this afternoon,' he said.

'To tell him I'd been pestering you already?'

He grinned. 'Something like that.'

'What did he say?'

'What do you think? I have to persuade you that whatever happened to your husband's plane it wasn't because of a manufacturing defect.'

'I've never thought there was anything wrong with the plane.' She paused. 'Actually that's not true. To begin with I half thought there might have been, but I don't now.'

He was disconcerted, not so much by her frankness, but because after everything she'd said, she now seemed willing to admit that Airtech were not to blame at all.

'Why are you making waves, then?' he asked.

'Because I have to find someone who'll help. I thought that if I made enough waves, as you put it, one of the newspapers in Australia could get interested, or Airtech might decide they'd better send someone to see me.'

'So I've made the whole damn trip for nothing,' Redman

said. 'Airtech are going to love this. Mrs Decker, I have to tell you – you should've waited for a journalist.'

She shook her head. 'I don't think so. Don't make up your mind yet.'

'Is it OK if I get angry?'

'I'd rather you didn't until you've heard what I have to say. Would you like more coffee or some whisky?'

'No, thank you.' He was surprised to find he wasn't angry. If anything he was intrigued. 'Why do you think I can help?' he said. 'You don't know me from a can of fish.'

'Are you married, Mr Redman?'

'No. Not anymore.'

'Oh.' She'd seen the change in his expression. 'I didn't mean to pry. I just wanted to explain that because of what happened to Warren – because of what I've found out – I have to do what I can to discover why he died – you know, because he was my husband.' She stopped speaking for a moment. 'That sounds dreadfully trite. I'm sorry. I thought it would be easier for you to understand if you had a wife – that's why I asked. Now it's all gone wrong because I've started off on the wrong foot again.'

'It's OK,' he said. 'I understand – at least I understand that bit. What I can't figure out is why you want a complete stranger to give you a hand. You must have friends here, and there has to be some kind of government authority who can start an inquiry if you don't think it was a straight accident.'

'My friends are all very sympathetic, Mr Redman, but this isn't Australia or the United States. I told you this afternoon: this is the Solomon Islands. Planes go missing all the time – small ones, I mean. Search and Rescue have better things to do than carry on investigating an accident that took place over a month ago, and the government have told me there is no justification for them to open an inquiry.' She sipped some wine from her glass. 'In a way I don't blame them. I can't prove anything.'

'But you don't believe your husband's plane went

down because of a storm or because of engine failure?'
She shook her head. 'No.'

'If you haven't been able to convince anyone else why
do you figure you can persuade me or some Australian
reporter you've never met before?'

'Because someone from overseas is likely to have more
imagination and a more open mind. People here are very
insular. The whole community is. It's not their fault; it's
just how things are in the islands. I thought that someone
from Airtech or a reporter would at least listen to me
without automatically assuming I was making up a story
to suit myself.' She put her wineglass back on the table.
'There's another reason, too. When I first started this, I
had a single piece of evidence – a few bits from Warren's
plane. It wasn't enough to get anyone interested and I
tried too hard. That made people think I was a crank.
Later, when I got more information and tried again, it was
too late. They'd already decided I'd become obsessed with
Warren's death, and that I was trying to find some
peculiar explanation for what was just an ordinary plane
crash.'

'You mean you needed to make a fresh start?' Redman
had been thinking while she spoke. 'Try your theory out
on someone you hadn't talked to before?'

'Hm. Except it's hardly a theory.'

By now he knew his assessment of Jennifer Decker was
correct. She had thought out her strategy with care and,
for a woman who had only recently lost her husband, she
was self-possessed and evidently confident of her ability
to gain his attention. Whether or not she could maintain
his interest remained to be seen, but already Redman was
inclined to believe she could.

'I have something to show you.' She pushed her chair
back from the table and stood up. 'In the other room.'

He followed her into what had obviously been Warren
Decker's office. A framed photograph of Decker sitting on
the wing of his Eagle hung on one wall, and on another,

there was a painting of an old biplane. A desk overflowing with charts, invoices and aviation magazines stood in the centre of the room.

'I'm sorry it's such a mess,' she said. 'I haven't got round to clearing it out yet.'

'Are you going to carry on living here?' he asked. 'In the islands?'

'No.' She shook her head. 'I didn't want to come to start with. It was Warren. We came to the Solomons three and a half years ago – after my uncle lent us the money to buy a new plane. Warren thought this was one of the only places left where there was a growing market for tourism and inter-island traffic. Before that he'd been working out of Adelaide with an old Piper Cherokee. I met him in Adelaide – we were married there.'

'You're Australian?' Redman said.

'Yes.' She knelt down and lifted something out of a cardboard box.

It was a seat squab from an Eagle, badly burned and encrusted in dried salt and soot.

'I had two of these,' she said. 'Some fishermen from Malaita found them floating way out at sea. They sent them over to a local islander called Jimmy Baura who gave them to me. Jimmy was a friend of Warren's.'

Redman took the squab from her, noticing that her hands were sprinkled with what looked like silver paint.

The dried salt wasn't salt and the silver paint wasn't silver paint. Instead the squab was impregnated with powder – fine, dry powder.

He banged the foam against his hand, making a small cloud of the powder jet out into the room.

'Particles of melted aluminium from the fuselage,' she said. 'Right?'

Redman met her eyes. 'Is that what you think?

She shook her head. 'Could it be that, though?'

'No.' He was certain. 'Not a chance.'

'There's black powder, too.' She pointed to the box.

'Most of it is in there.'

In the bottom of the box there was a dusting of silver, and a lesser quantity of what Redman thought was soot. He smeared some of the darker powder into the palm of his hand.

'I don't know,' he said. 'I can't see why a floating seat squab should have any of this on it, or in it.'

For the first time since he'd met her, she seemed nervous. Under the make-up her cheeks were flushed and she was twiddling the end of her belt with her fingers.

'Where's the other squab?'

'The one you're holding is the one I took around to show people. It was in the trunk of my car when someone broke into the house one day while I was out. They took half my jewellery, thirty-eight dollars in cash and the other squab. It was in the box, right here.'

He smiled. 'Real convincing. You've no idea why they took it?'

'Only that it could have something to do with the crash. But the burglary was what made me go back to talk to Jimmy. He spent five days on Malaita talking to the fishermen and some of the islanders there. Jimmy's a very kind person, so is his wife. They've been tremendous to me.'

'And?' Redman said.

She took the squab and returned it to the box. 'According to Jimmy, two of the fishermen think they saw Warren's plane explode or what could have made the plane explode. They were on a boat, way out to sea, miles and miles away. They said it was lightning – the biggest flash of lightning they'd ever seen. It caused a *tsunami* – you know, a tidal wave – just a little one.'

'Was there a storm?'

'No. Dead calm day, high cloud and absolutely no wind. They didn't see any more lightning, either.' She paused. 'That's not all.'

'Go on,' Redman said.

'The fishermen remembered seeing a smaller lightning flash a few days earlier. Each time afterwards there was a lot of this black and silver powder floating on the sea. They even collected some in a jar because it was so unusual.'

Although his curiosity was growing, Redman knew the powder could have come from anywhere. From what she'd said, there was no evidence to prove Decker's plane had flown into a cloud of it, or that the powder had ever been airborne. Even if it had settled out from the air, it could be atmospheric dust from a volcanic eruption thousands of miles away and have nothing to do with either the lightning or the disappearance of her husband's plane.

'Pretty weird,' he said.

'It gets weirder.' She unfolded a map. On it someone had drawn a line in red ink between two of the major islands. Redman guessed it showed Decker's flight route.

'I think Warren's plane went down here.' She pointed to a dot some distance from the line. 'That's where the fishermen saw the lightning. That means he was a long way out in the Pacific – well off what would be a normal course from San Cristobal to Malaita.'

'Lousy place to ditch,' he said.

'Or catch fire.' She took a pen and drew a small circle on the east coast of Malaita, half-way down the island. 'This is what I wanted to tell Mr Hawthorne – why I phoned him. Somewhere around here there's an old World War II airstrip. It's all overgrown and no one uses it because there's no land access. There aren't any roads, only a river. Most people don't even know it's there.'

'But you do?' he said.

'I do now. I didn't until a few days ago. Jimmy told me about it when he came back. He hasn't been to the airstrip himself but the mountain people he spoke to on Malaita said they'd seen Europeans there – over the last couple of months.'

Redman remained silent, waiting for her to continue.

'The Malaitans think they were from a Taiwanese squid boat that was anchored offshore round about the same time. That's strange enough, but not as strange as the name the Malaitans had for the men.' She glanced at him. 'They called them the white men with the silver water.'

He looked at the dark streak on his palm and at the flecks of silver still adhering to his skin. 'Is that it?' he said.

She nodded. 'I know what you're going to say. Don't ask me what theory I have to explain all of this. I can't explain any of it. If I could, I wouldn't be asking for your help.'

'There's nothing else?'

'No. Not really.' She appeared worried. 'I thought it would be—' Her voice tailed off.

'Can we go back to the other room?'

'Of course. I'm sorry.' She brushed past him, deliberately avoiding his eyes.

As well as enjoying her company, over the course of the evening Redman had been unable to avoid studying Jennifer Decker in some detail. She was quite attractive, he thought, rather like a woodland nymph or perhaps a painting of one – a girl disguised as a woman. In a way she reminded him of Josie.

'Can I get you some more coffee?' she enquired.

'No, thanks.'

He sat down, knowing already that plain curiosity wasn't going to be enough. It didn't matter whether he liked her, or how curious he was about her story. The dullness would always be there, the same emptiness that had taken the colour out of everything for the past two years.

'You're going to turn me down, aren't you?' She spoke quietly.

'I've got a friend in Brisbane. I'll talk to him.'

'Oh.' She tried to conceal her disappointment. 'But you do believe me – about it not being an accident?'

'I don't know.' Redman hesitated. 'I just think it's going

to be too hard to find out anything that makes sense. I'm sorry. I really am. If I thought I could do any good, I'd do it.' He stood up. 'I'd better go, it's getting late.'

'I'm sorry, too.' She collected her car keys from a bowl on the table. 'I'll run you back to your hotel.'

'I can call a taxi.'

'It's all right. I like driving in the dark.' She was biting her lip, trying to maintain her composure. 'It was nice of you to come, anyway.'

Redman was part way out of the front door when he saw a figure duck into the shadows across the street.

'There was someone by your car,' he said. 'Over there – a man.'

'He's been around on and off for the last four days.'

'You didn't say anything about that.'

'No.' She glanced at him. 'Does it make any difference?'

'Hell, I don't know.' He was annoyed now, partly with himself and partly because she hadn't mentioned it before.

He climbed into the car feeling inconsiderate and confused.

As she had done on the drive from the airport, for the entire trip back to the hotel she remained silent, sitting tight-lipped behind the wheel, clearly unwilling to reopen the coversation.

For Jennifer Decker, an evening of hope had turned into an evening of lost opportunity. Either her opinion of Redman had been wrong, or her attempt to solicit his help had been as ineffectual as she had feared it might be. Now, with the evening gone, she could think of no excuse to contact him again.

She parked the car outside the hotel, keeping the engine running while Redman thanked her for dinner and said goodbye.

'I'll call you if I turn up anything,' he said.

She made sure he couldn't see her face when he closed the door, and was careful not to drive away too fast.

Not until she was clear of the hotel lights did the feeling of weakness and despair start to overtake her. And only then did the tears begin rolling down her cheeks.

Had she known what was confronting Redman in his hotel room while she was driving home, she would have been less certain of her failure, and less inclined to believe the evening had been wasted.

The moment he'd unlocked his door, Redman knew what had happened. From one end of the room to the other there was a trail of empty drawers, coathangers, pieces of clothing and overturned cupboards. Even the bed had been stripped bare.

He stood now in the middle of the mess, trying to comprehend how an unwanted visit to the Solomon Islands could turn into such a puzzle in such a short time.

That the search of his room was somehow connected with his visit to the Decker home tonight seemed beyond doubt. But an explanation for the search, was another matter altogether, he thought. What the hell were they looking for? Had they found it?

He returned to the downstairs foyer and asked the girl if there was somewhere he could get a drink.

'The Polynesian Club is still open.' She leaned across the desk and pointed. 'Through there.'

The bar was crowded with Europeans and a number of well-dressed islanders. None of them looked up or showed any interest at his presence.

He bought a half-bottle of bourbon then retreated to his room for some serious thinking.

By two o'clock in the morning, with most of the bourbon gone, Redman had made his decision. He thumbed through the phone book until he found the number, dialling it quickly before he could reconsider.

'Hello.' Jennifer Decker answered on the second ring.

'This is Steve Redman. I'm sorry to wake you up.'

'That's all right. Did you leave something behind?'

'No. I've been thinking – about what you told me.'

'Oh.'

'Listen, could I talk to this Jimmy Baura guy?'

'Yes, I suppose so. What for?'

'Well, you went to a lot of trouble faxing Airtech, talking to Hawthorne, trying to get me over here, explaining everything.' Redman faltered. 'And I've got this report to write.'

'Has something happened, Mr Redman?'

'Nothing serious. I just kind of figured I shouldn't have been so rude this evening.'

'You weren't rude.' Her voice brightened. 'You haven't changed your mind, have you?'

'No promises,' he said.

'I don't expect promises.'

'OK. Can we see Jimmy Baura in the morning?'

'All right. I'll pick you up. We'll have to drive up the coast – to Cape Esperance.'

'Not too early,' he said. 'I need to call this friend of mine in Brisbane – the one I mentioned. It's getting a bit late to try now.'

'Mr Redman?'

'Yeah.'

'Thank you for calling me. I'm more grateful than you can imagine.'

'My pleasure.' He said goodbye, convinced now that he had been right, and surprised how easily he'd been able to make the decision.

This way, Redman thought, if it turns out to be a wild goose chase, at least it wasn't someone in California making the decision for him.

The breakthrough was refreshing, so much so that he spent some minutes looking for the chloroquine tablets she'd given him. A precaution, he told himself, in case his visit was to become more than a two-day break from the office.

He swallowed the tablets, washing them down with what remained of the bourbon. Then he lay down on the bed to begin his pre-sleep ritual of erasing all the memories of Josie from his mind.

Two

Redman's breakfast arrived before he'd finished putting his room back together. He went to the door and let the waiter in.

'Good morning. You have a good sleep, sir?' The waiter was Melanesian, a stocky man wearing carved wooden bracelets on his wrists.

'I got started kind of late.' Redman removed some coathangers from the table to make space for the tray. 'Can you tell me how far Cape Esperance is from here?'

'One hour, maybe less. You are diving on the reef?'

'No,' Redman said. 'Just a trip with a friend.' He handed over a five-dollar Solomon Island note. 'Thanks for the breakfast.'

When the waiter had gone, Redman buttered two pieces of toast, munching on them while he completed his housekeeping. As far as he could make out, nothing was missing. The contents of his brief-case had been tipped on to the floor; the fax from Hawthorne had been removed from his diary and someone had been through his clothes to see if anything was hidden inside them. Other than that, there were no clues to indicate what the intruders had been after.

He poured himself a cup of coffee, then sat down on the bed to make his call to Owen Mitchell.

There was a click of an answering machine followed by the beginning of a recorded message. It was interrupted by Owen's voice.

'Good-day,' Redman said. 'This is Steve. Why have you got your machine on if you're home?'

'Forgot to switch it off last night. I thought you were going overseas.'

'I am overseas. I'm calling from Honiara.'

'Do they have telephones there?'

'Listen,' Redman said patiently, 'I need a favour.'

'What kind of favour?'

'I want you to start thinking about something.' Redman spoke for several minutes without stopping, outlining the background to his meeting with Jennifer Decker, before going on to describe the powder in the Eagle's seat squab.

'Have you got that?' Redman asked.

'Yes, I've got it. Why should I be able to figure it out? Am I supposed to be clairvoyant or something?'

'I'll bring a sample of the powder back with me.'

'Stick some in an envelope and airmail it.'

'There's no point,' Redman said. 'I'll be back in Brisbane before it arrives. I'll see you when I get home. How much do you need?'

'Anything from a teaspoonful to a couple of tons. Depends what it is.'

Redman hung up. Any conversation with Owen was an endurance test, but there was no one better qualified to solve the mystery of the powder, he thought. If Owen couldn't find any explanation, Jennifer Decker might as well give up.

He drank a second cup of coffee, and was contemplating a third when the phone rang.

It was a girl from the front desk, calling to say that a Mrs Decker was waiting for him in the downstairs lounge.

She was sitting in a corner by the window, reading a

newspaper.

'Morning,' Redman said.

'Oh, hello.' She stood up. 'I'm not too early, am I?'

'No, of course not.' He wondered if he should tell her about the search of his room.

'Did you call your friend?'

'I just finished talking to him, a minute ago. He's going to have to think about things.'

'Do you believe he'll come up with any ideas? About the powder, I mean.'

'Yes, I do. Owen's pretty smart. He works for the university in Brisbane – or he does when he feels like it. As long as I've managed to get him interested he'll dig around until he finds the answer. If he can't find it, no one can.'

'Is that true, Mr Redman, or are you being optimistic?'

'Both.' He smiled at her. 'Suppose you call me Steve so I can call you Jennifer.'

She returned his smile. 'Your Mr Hawthorne wouldn't like it. When I spoke to him on the phone he said Airtech would only discuss things with me at arm's length.'

'Come on.' Redman led her from the lounge. 'Don't worry about Hawthorne.'

Outside the hotel the heat was coming off the ground in waves. Although she'd parked her car in the shade, it took nearly ten minutes for the air-conditioning unit to reduce the temperature to a reasonable level, and it was several more minutes before Redman started to feel anything like comfortable. By then, the Nissan was travelling west on the main road out of Honiara, taking him into territory he hadn't seen before.

Yesterday, after his trip into town, he'd started to believe that the island was more developed than he'd thought. Now, he realized his first impression had been right. Honiara was uncharacteristic, a pocket of civilization on an island that otherwise consisted of nothing but coconut plantations, rivers, jungle and deserted beaches.

'Can you drive all round the coast?' he asked.

'Heavens, no.' She laughed. 'Once you get to the Cape the road only goes on for about another twenty miles – to Lambi Bay. After that you have to walk, and you really need a guide. There are crocodiles in the Variana river – big ones.'

'What about the other islands?'

'Santa Ysabel, Choiseul and San Cristobal hardly have any roads at all.' She glanced at him. 'You have to be a certain kind of person to put up with living in the Solomons. There used to be headhunters on Santa Ysabel at a place called Roviana. They killed off a lot of people up in the north-east corner of the island.'

'Great for tourists,' Redman said. 'What about this island with the airstrip on it?'

'Malaita's different – mostly because of the islanders who live there. No one likes them. They don't even like each other. The mountain people don't get on with the villagers on the coast. Warren never managed to make friends with any Malaitans.'

'But he made friends with this guy Jimmy?'

She nodded. 'Jimmy was born here on Guadalcanal – so was Louise – that's his wife. They both work up at the Tambea Village Resort. Warren had a business contract with the resort – you know, flying visitors around for sightseeing. That's how he met Jimmy.'

The Solomons would be a tough place for a woman, Redman thought. He was surprised someone like Jennifer Decker had been prepared to live here for so long.

Abandoning his speculation, he settled back to think instead about how to write the report for Hawthorne.

They had been travelling for nearly fifty minutes when Jennifer swung the car on to a narrow track between some trees. The track opened out to a clearing, at the back of which stood a small wooden building. It was unpainted with a corrugated-iron roof, but it had glass in the windows and a fly screen over the front door. It also had a large radio aerial bolted to one of the outside walls.

In what had once been a garden, a number of hens were scratching around. Nearby was a pig, tethered by its leg to a concrete block.

Parking a safe distance from the pig, Jennifer sounded the horn.

The islander who came to meet them was over six feet tall. He was a dark-skinned, well-built man with fair hair and features that were more European than Melanesian.

Redman followed Jennifer over to say hello.

'This is Steve Redman.' She introduced him. 'He's a friend.'

The Solomon islander studied Redman carefully. 'You are Australian?' he said.

'No. I'm an American.' Redman shook hands.

'American Indian?'

'No. Not a proper one. My grandfather was half Cherokee. That's where the name comes from.'

'Ah.' A grin spread over Jimmy's face. 'You're a mixture, like me. Many years ago my own grandfather comes here from Scotland. One day in bed with my grandmother he makes a bad mistake, I think.'

'I bet he didn't tell you that.' Redman smiled. 'If I'd ever asked my grandfather if he thought it was a mistake he'd have given me a hiding.'

'We shall drink beer together. My wife she works at the resort today so it is good for me to have company. While we drink, Mrs Decker will tell me why you have come. Please to enter my home where it is not so hot.'

It was a good deal cooler inside. The house lay in the shade of several large trees, and an off-shore breeze was coming through the bamboo blinds.

Redman accepted a can of beer. It was warm but he barely noticed. He had enjoyed the drive up the coast and, despite being in unfamiliar surroundings, he felt remarkably at ease. He sipped at his beer, listening to Jennifer explain the reason for their visit.

'You have many questions?' Jimmy enquired.

'Not a lot,' Redman said. 'Tell me about this airstrip on Malaita. I know you haven't seen it, but you're certain Europeans have been there, are you?'

Jimmy shrugged. 'Europeans, Americans, I do not know which.'

'But they weren't Taiwanese?'

'I ask the Malaitans this. They say round eyes – white man's eyes.'

'But the islanders still think the men came off a Taiwanese boat?' Redman said.

'Yes.' Jimmy hesitated. 'You understand there are no tourists on that part of Malaita. There is no reason for white men to be in such a place.'

'Unless they had something to do with the powder,' Jennifer interrupted. 'And that was what brought down Warren's plane.'

'If it did,' Redman said. 'Jimmy, do you think there's any chance the islanders saw the name of the boat? Or a number on it?'

'I did not ask them. But there was an old man who has taken a canoe out to the boat one night. He looks for the garbage which is thrown overboard. Sometimes there are things the islanders can use. He may know the name.'

'The airstrip's probably more important,' Redman said. 'Do these mountain people have any idea what was going on there?'

'They will not talk to me about it.'

'Why?'

'Maybe they are told not to speak with strangers – by the white men.'

Jennifer put down her beer can. 'You didn't say anything about that before,' she said.

'You ask me only what I know. I do not wish to guess what has happened to Mr Decker.'

'What is your guess, Jimmy?' Redman said. 'Your best guess.'

'I think these men from the boat make the lightning,

and it is the lightning which makes Mr Decker's plane crash into the sea.'

Redman wished he hadn't asked. The conclusion was no different to his own, an almost inescapable conclusion, even if it was based on a jumble of facts that didn't make sense.

'I take you to the airstrip, yes?' Jimmy passed him another can of beer. 'So you can look.'

'I don't know.' He was unwilling to commit himself. The visit had not added materially to what Jennifer had already said, and a trip to Malaita could prove equally fruitless.

Jennifer stood up. 'We could do it in a couple of days,' she said. 'Fly to Auki tomorrow, take a car up to Fouia and then go round by boat.'

'How did you get to talk to the mountain people, Jimmy?' Redman asked.

'I go first on the *Compass Rose*. It is a coastal trader which takes passengers to Auki. Then I cross the island by following two rivers. For Mrs Decker, it is not possible to make such a journey.' Jimmy grinned. 'Even for an Indian it is too difficult, I think.'

'I can't see much point in going,' Redman said. 'The squid boat isn't there anymore; the white men have disappeared – whoever the hell they were – and if the Malaitans won't talk to Jimmy, they're not going to talk to me, are they?'

Jennifer swung round to face him. 'I'll pay you,' she said. 'I'll pay you a thousand dollars – American dollars.'

'I'm already getting paid.' Her offer had caught him off balance. 'You don't have to bribe me for Christ's sake.'

'You give some dollars to me,' Jimmy said. 'I use it to make the islanders talk.'

Redman tried to imagine himself back in Brisbane, back in his nice cool office with his visit to the Solomons over. Would he regret leaving the job half done? A month from now – a year from now – how hard would it be to forget the expression on Jennifer Decker's face as she'd offered him the money, to forget the search of his room and the man outside her house last night?

'Mr Redman.' She intruded on his thoughts. 'Steve.'

'All right, all right,' he said. 'You don't have to bang me over the head.'

Again he had found it easy to make up his mind, and again he had no reason to question his decision. Drinking warm beer in the comfort of Jimmy Baura's home, Redman was too busy with the present to consider where the decision might lead and, for the moment, the warning bells in his head were still too faint for him to hear them.

Rising over the mountains to the east, the sun was washing the whole of Malaita with light. Already the rain forest was less forbidding, and the mist which had been drifting out of the valleys was dispersing into clear blue sunshine.

If Redman had ever harboured any illusions about the remoteness of Malaita, the thirty-minute Solair flight from Honiara to Auki had dispelled them. This morning he had disembarked not at a terminal, but at a shed on the edge of a timeless Solomon Island village of thatched huts on stilts where the aroma of cooking fires blended with the odour of moist vegetation, and where the laughter of children mixed with the barking of dogs to create an atmosphere quite unlike anything he had experienced before.

Standing now at the harbour side, Redman was enjoying being here as much as he was looking forward to the day ahead.

'You know, I can understand why some Europeans want to live in the South Pacific,' he said. 'It's not the same as anywhere else, is it?'

'No.' Jennifer shook her head. 'Warren loved it. Because it's so unsophisticated, I suppose. I've never got used to it. I've never wanted to.'

Today she was wearing jeans, leather boots and a safari jacket. Redman thought it made her look even more like a schoolgirl.

'Is there something the matter?' she asked.

'No.' Redman concentrated his attention on a fishing boat which was making its way towards them.

Smoking heavily from the exhaust, the boat was about thirty feet long, and from a distance, appeared to be somewhat dilapidated. In the wheel-house, standing legs apart, was the unmistakable figure of Jimmy Baura. He guided the boat up to the wharf, throwing a rope around a bollard once he was alongside.

Redman clambered aboard carrying the box of supplies and the roll of sleeping-bags before he reached out to help Jennifer on to the deck. The boat smelt strongly of fish, but it was clean enough inside and seemed to have been moderately well looked after.

'How much?' Redman asked.

'For two days, four hundred Solomon Island dollars,' Jimmy said. 'Two hundred American. It is OK?'

'Sure.'

'The money buys the diesel also,' Jimmy said. 'I fill the tank already. It is good we travel by boat. The fisherman I hire it from say the rains have washed out the north road in two places this side of Malu'u. With a four-wheel-drive truck it is passable but it would take us much time.'

'You don't have to talk me into it,' Redman said. 'The boat's great. It doesn't look too fast, that's all.'

'By sea it will take us less than twelve hours to reach the airstrip. Last time, when I come and cross the island by foot, I am climbing and walking for nearly three days.' Jimmy wiped some oil off his hands. 'You wish to start?'

'Whenever you're ready,' Redman said. 'You're the captain. Do you want me to cast off?'

'I do it.' Jimmy went forward to release the rope, pushing the hull away from the wharf with his feet before he returned to take the wheel.

He opened the throttle, then, as the boat began to move, struck a pose of dignified authority. 'Mrs Decker,' he said. 'Please, you will take a photograph – for Louise.'

Jennifer laughed. 'Captain Baura at the helm of....' She stopped. 'Oh, I don't know what the name is.'

Redman made his way to the bow and peered over the side. 'The *Kwaibala*,' he called.

He remained on the foredeck, watching the coast slip away, pleased to be at sea in a part of the world he had not expected to visit. Off the starboard bow, Malaita had again assumed the appearance of a desolate, inhospitable chunk of land. Morning shadows being cast by the mountains imparted an almost mystical quality to the island, and even though the sun was higher now, Redman could not quite overcome the feeling that this was a place where he would never feel at home.

Standing inside the wheel-house, Jennifer Decker's reaction to the island was one of indifference. For three and a half years she had struggled to come to terms with the Solomons, knowing how wrong her husband had been to bring her here. She also knew that if his death had not released her from an environment she had never been able to accept, her marriage would have soon been over. It was her recognition of this – her belief that she had somehow failed him – which had created the need to find a reason for his accident.

It had prolonged her stay in Honiara, but now Redman was here – now the investigation was being taken over by someone more capable than she could ever be – her responsibilities were nearly at an end. Soon, she thought, the worst of the guilt would surely begin to disappear.

She touched Jimmy's shoulder. 'I'm going to talk to Steve,' she said. 'You don't mind, do you?'

'You say to Mr Redman we have a beer soon. Before it gets too rough.' Jimmy pointed ahead to some white caps. 'The wind is changing. we must reach the other side of the island before it gets better, I think.'

She removed her boots and her socks, leaving them in the wheel-house before clambering barefoot to the bow.

'Hi.' She sat down beside Redman. 'Jimmy wants a beer with you.'

'I'll make him wait for lunch.'

'Are you glad you came now? To the Solomons, I mean.'

Redman looked at her. 'Was I that bad tempered when I got off the plane?'

'Mm. You're all right now, though.'

'This is a bit of a change from an office job. It takes a while to wind down.' He wiped some spray out of his eyes. 'I like this. Maybe I ought to buy the *Kwaibala* and live on a beach somewhere.'

'That's what Warren thought – except he bought a plane. He'd have been happy to stay out here for the rest of his life – even if it was by himself.' She hesitated. 'How long were you married?'

'Four months.'

'Oh.' She was annoyed with herself for asking. 'I'm sorry.'

'It's OK.'

'Do you really believe we'll find something at the airstrip?'

'If I didn't, you and I wouldn't be taking a cruise around some island that seems to consist entirely of rocks and forest.' He smiled at her. 'It's pretty wild, isn't it?'

She nodded, uncertain of what to say next, wondering why sometimes she felt comfortable talking to him when, on other occasions, she was conscious of him looking at her. Today he was in neutral, she thought, neither preoccupied with himself nor interested in her.

The *Kwaibala* was further out from shore now, pushing through an increasingly choppy sea towards the Lau lagoon at the top of the island. When the spray started breaking over the bow in waves, Jennifer retreated to the wheel-house. Redman followed shortly afterwards. There they settled down for the remainder of the journey north and the long haul down the east coast.

At midday, Jennifer served sandwiches and coffee, spilling most of the drinks over herself as she tried to keep her footing on a pitching deck. Not until late afternoon did conditions improve and the white caps begin to die away.

By four o'clock, with the wind much reduced and the sea very nearly flat, they were making better headway than at any time since leaving Auki. On the shelf beside the wheel, a row of empty beer cans marked their progress south in thirty-minute intervals – a navigational aid which Jimmy claimed would allow him to calculate their time of arrival to the nearest half a can. Redman was less confident. According to Jimmy, the river-mouth would be the only certain way to pin-point the location of the airstrip, but with dozens of rivers streaming out of the mountains along every mile of coastline, picking out the right one would not be easy.

In the end it was not the river-mouth which led them to the airstrip but the airstrip itself, a gap in the jungle which could be seen from the decks of the *Kwaibala* some minutes before there was any sign of the river.

'I tell you, I am a pretty good captain, eh?' Jimmy was pleased with himself. 'There you see it now.'

On the south side of the clearing, flanked by mangroves, the river delta was nearly a hundred yards wide, a flat area of muddy water emerging from a rock-strewn valley. Some of the rocks were the size of a small car. It was an unlikely spot for anyone to have built a landing-strip, Redman thought, even in wartime.

'Can you see anything?' he asked Jennifer.

She was looking through the telephoto lens of her camera, steadying herself against the side of the cabin.

'Not yet. Just some old buildings at the far end.'

Jimmy turned the bow of the *Kwaibala*, then throttled back the engine, heading cautiously for the mangroves and towards what appeared to be a concrete ramp.

Although the water was growing muddier by the minute, Redman was fairly sure it was deep enough for them to anchor. He went forward to check, leaving Jimmy to edge the *Kwaibala* closer. A moment later Redman jumped on to the ramp.

He felt curiously excited, as though he was stepping back in history to a place that had remained undisturbed since the end of the war.

The feeling was short lived. Steel rings set into the concrete exhibited evidence of recent use, and the surface of the ramp was covered in fresh skid marks from a rubber-tyred vehicle.

He tied the *Kwaibala*'s mooring rope to one of the rings, waiting for Jennifer to disembark. She too had seen the tyre marks.

'Tractor,' she said.

'Or something like it.' Redman drew his foot across one of the marks. 'With a load on. The driver burned a lot of rubber getting up here.'

Jimmy cut the motor and came to join them on the ramp. 'We look around now,' he said. 'Then I leave you here. Before it is dark I travel into the hills.'

'Can't you wait until tomorrow?' Jennifer said.

'Tomorrow we leave again for our return to Auki.' Jimmy turned to Redman. 'You give me some dollars for the islanders, yes?'

'Sure.' Redman handed him a roll of bills.

'OK.' Jimmy started off up the ramp.

'Wait a second.' Jennifer gave Redman her camera to hold. 'I'd better fetch my boots. I'm not walking round in the jungle with nothing on my feet.'

While she was away, Redman asked Jimmy how long he'd be gone.

'I come back here in the morning.' The islander paused. 'You look after Mrs Decker.'

Redman knew the remark was made seriously. 'I will,' he said. 'Do you think we should sleep on the boat?'

'It is better because of the mosquitoes and the centipedes.'

'Centipedes?'

'They come out at night.' Jimmy stuck out his hands. 'Bastards this big. Perhaps one foot long.'

'We'll sleep on board,' Redman said. 'Maybe we should stay on board.'

Jimmy grinned again. 'First we make our search.'

A search of the airstrip proved unnecessary. The evidence was everywhere.

Jennifer found it first. She had returned from the boat carrying her boots, but had not bothered to put them on until she climbed to the top of the ramp. While she was kneeling down she came across the powder. It was trapped in a crack, flecks of powder glittering in the sunshine like fragments of a broken mirror.

Redman went to look for more, realizing at once that there was no need. The rains had washed traces of powder into just about every crack in the concrete. In the grass at the edge of the runway there were pockets of it.

The sheer quantity was proof enough for Redman. He was certain now that the particles in the Eagle's seat squab had originally come from here. How it had got to the airstrip to start with was less clear, but the squid boat was the most likely explanation, he thought. Although why a Taiwanese squid boat should have carried a cargo of black and silver powder to a deserted airstrip on the east coast of Malaita, he could not begin to imagine.

'Steve,' Jennifer called to him. She was picking up something.

He went to see what she'd found, but stopped before he reached her. All around him the runway was streaked with rubber. Unlike the marks on the ramp, these were narrower and more distinct. There were fifty or sixty of them, overlapping parallel lines cutting across the mosaic of grass-filled cracks at the end of the strip nearest to the sea.

The answer had been staring him in the face. He'd known all along, he realized. Ever since Jennifer had told him about this place. Coming here had just confirmed it.

'Look.' She handed him a thin metal tube. It was about two inches long with a pair of coloured wires protruding from one end. 'Do you know what it is?'

He put it in his pocket, too busy thinking to reply.

'Steve, what's the matter?'

'Dusters,' Redman said. 'Goddamn dusters. I should've thought of it before.'

'I don't understand.'

'Crop-dusters. Fixed-wing aircraft for spraying pesticides or dropping fertilizer. Someone has been flying crop dusters out of here.' He pointed to the streaks on the runway. 'Those are landing marks – aircraft wheel marks.'

Her eyes widened. 'Dust. You mean they've been dropping it from the air.'

'Yep.'

'And Warren flew into a cloud of it?'

'Maybe.' Redman paused. 'That's what I can't figure out. If you're right about where his plane went down – where the fishermen say they saw the lightning – there's no way your husband could have flown into it.'

'Why not?'

'Because it's impossible to fly a crop duster that far out into the Pacific – not with a load on. Some of them carry nearly a ton. That gives them a lousy range. You don't need much range for crop dusting.'

'Oh.' She frowned. 'Suppose a cloud of dust was blown out to sea.'

'You said there wasn't any wind that day. Anyway, it wouldn't stay airborne. Sooner or later it would settle out on the water and eventually sink.'

She put her hands on her hips. 'So how did it get into the seat squab? Why has someone been flying crop dusters off this airstrip?'

'I don't know.' Redman smiled at her. 'Not yet.'

'What about the tube thing I gave you?'

He took it from his pocket. ' It's a detonator – for setting off an explosive charge.'

'Can you make a cloud of dust explode?' Her head was filled with questions. They were coming faster than she could ask them.

'I don't think so.' Redman had been wrestling with the problem. 'Maybe. I'm not sure. It's not like a cloud of gas or some kind of liquid like gasoline. You can make gasoline explode if it's atomized into fine droplets, but this isn't liquid – it's powder, or dust.'

'Steve....' She began to ask him something else but stopped when he held up a hand.

'Take it easy,' he said. 'We'll find out what it is; why someone has been spraying it around in this Godforsaken place, and whether it has anything to do with the plane crash. Just hold on until we've had more of a look round and had a bit more time to think.'

'It has to have something to do with Warren's accident. You know it has.'

'All we know is that the seats from the Eagle had some of this dust on them. Dust will float for a long time – so will a seat squab.'

'You're not trying to connect things together.' Her eyes were flashing. 'And you're patronizing me. You think this is a game, some sort of puzzle that you won't try to solve unless you have all the pieces.'

'We sure as hell won't solve it with the information we've got so far,' Redman said. 'Stop being so impatient. I'm going to tell Jimmy about the aircraft. He can ask the Malaitans if they saw them.'

The islander had gone exploring by himself. He was at the far end of the runway near the huts when Redman caught up with him.

'I go soon,' Jimmy said. 'It is getting late.'

'Listen to this first.' Redman gave him a run-down on the crop dusters, describing what they looked like.

'I ask the mountain people,' Jimmy said. 'Perhaps if they have not seen them, they hear the engines. It is very quiet here. In the war, I think the Americans only find this airstrip by listening for noise.'

'Was this built by the Japanese?'

Jimmy nodded. 'In the jungle I find barbed wire and an old machine-gun post. The gun is still there. It is a Japanese gun, but very rusty.'

'Have you been inside the huts yet?'

'No. I wait for you.' Jimmy walked into the shell of a derelict, corrugated-iron building, and started kicking over the debris on the floor.

Redman was more methodical, searching for tell-tale signs of visitors. The tyre marks and the detonators were give-aways, he thought, but there had to be other clues as well.

He found them in the third hut. Of the four that remained standing, it was the only one with a roof, or part of a roof. The walls were sheets of perforated rust, it had no doors, no windows and the steel framing was eaten away to almost nothing. The dirt floor, though, had been swept clean. And on it, scattered around, were the signs Redman had hoped would be here.

There were rows of empty fifty-gallon drums, cardboard boxes, gas cylinders, ant-infested cans, bottles and even a half-used roll of toilet paper. In an empty cigarette packet he found another detonator.

He was picking through more of the rubbish when Jennifer arrived.

'Guess where most of this came from,' he said.

'Where?' She knew he wouldn't have asked if the answer was Taiwan.

'Either Hong Kong or Australia.' Redman tossed her an empty bean can. 'Have a look.'

She read the label before going to drop the can into one of the drums. 'There's powder in here,' she said. 'Dust, I mean.'

Redman checked two other drums. Both had dust residue lying in the bottom and adhering to the sides.

His examination was interrupted by Jimmy who was clearly anxious to get away.

'Tomorrow, please you will be ready to leave before ten o'clock,' he said.

'OK.' Leaving Jennifer in the hut, Redman accompanied the islander to the mouth of the delta.

The river was clearer here, a white torrent of water swirling between rocks and tree roots before it fanned out into the quieter delta flats. Jimmy fastened a sweat band around his forehead, said goodbye to Redman and began his climb. In less than a minute he had disappeared into the jungle.

It was cooler now, with the sun already low over the mountain ridge to the west. In the trees along the airstrip, flocks of birds were beginning to assemble. They fluttered noisily among the leaves, squabbling over the best places to roost.

Redman walked back to the hut, considering his own arrangements for spending the night. On board the *Kwaibala* it would be too stuffy to sleep below, but there would be no privacy for Jennifer if they both bunked down together in the wheel-house. Not that she'd care, he decided. He understood her better now – even to the point where he had concluded that her determination had little to do with her husband's disappearance and everything to do with some facet of her own personality. Perhaps tonight she might unwind, he thought. And if she did, perhaps he would be able to learn more about her.

He put the idea to the back of his mind, occupying himself by getting her to photograph the wheel marks and the contents of the hut before the light faded any further.

It was dusk by the time they made their way back to the ramp. The birds had stopped their noise, and apart from the sounds of waves lapping against the hull of the *Kwaibala*, the sea and the jungle were silent.

While Jennifer was taking a photo of the mangroves, Redman heard the throb of an engine.

'Listen.' He touched her arm.

She lowered her camera. 'It's a boat. Coming up the coast.'

It was a launch, a large game-fishing boat, rounding the headland on the south bank of the delta.

Redman watched it turn and saw the bow dip as it reduced speed.

'Visitors,' he said.

'Maybe they're going to anchor in the river overnight.'

'Maybe.'

'No one knows we're here,' Jennifer said uneasily.

'Well they do now.'

The launch was fifty yards away, travelling slowly towards the ramp. A man shouted a greeting to them from the foredeck.

Redman did not respond. He could see at least two other men on board.

'What are we going to do?' Jennifer whispered.

Redman considered his options. On such a deserted stretch of coast, the arrival of the launch was no coincidence. That was clear. But why it had arrived was a mystery. He waited for it to tie up alongside the *Kwaibala*, then made up his mind.

'Stay here,' he said. 'I'm going to say hello. If anything happens, you take off. Follow the river back into the jungle as far as you can go, and stay there. It'll be dark in a few minutes.'

'What about you?' She stared at him.

'Just do what I say.'

Redman walked part way down the ramp to meet a tall man who had disembarked from the launch. He was dressed in white trousers and a white open-necked shirt.

'Well, hello there,' he said.

Redman said nothing. Nor did he make any attempt to shake hands.

'Mr Redman, I presume.' The man spoke with a pronounced British accent. 'Mr Steven Redman from Airtech in Brisbane. Is that correct?'

'What do you want?' Redman said. He could feel his heart beating.

The man glanced up the ramp. 'And your lady friend is Mrs Decker, I imagine.'

'Look,' Redman said, 'you can presume and imagine what you like. I'm kind of busy. If you've made a special trip here to say something – say it.'

'How commendably direct.' The man beckoned to a companion on board the launch.

By now, Redman knew this was not a social visit. He began to retreat. When he saw what the man on the launch was carrying he began to run.

Waiting nervously at the top of the ramp, Jennifer had yet to move. Redman yelled at her, grabbed her hand, and started sprinting off down the airstrip pulling her along behind him.

She tried to keep up, close to losing her balance at every step because he would neither slacken speed nor release her hand.

They had made nearly eighty yards when Redman heard the clamour of the machine-gun. At the same time the first bullets zipped past his right knee, smashing into the runway.

Fragments of lead and chips of concrete bit into his legs as he began to weave, hauling Jennifer from one side to the other in a frantic bid to keep her moving.

Ahead stood the row of derelict huts. Beyond them lay the jungle, the river and the rocks. He chose the rocks, heading for the only cover that would give them the slightest chance.

Two-thirds of the way there, with the bullets still coming and with his breath rasping in his throat, Redman made a final effort.

It was not enough. A few yards from safety there was a

prolonged burst of fire. He felt Jennifer's hand slip from his grasp, saw her stumble and saw her fling out her arms before she hit the concrete.

He dragged her the rest of the way, towing her by her wrists like a broken doll until he reached the shelter of one of the larger boulders. He lay her down there, relieved to find she was still breathing.

Behind them the machine-gun had stopped. For a few precious seconds he could afford to pause, gulp some air, and attend to Jennifer before he carried her on up the river to find somewhere they could hide. Then all he had to do was keep her alive until Jimmy came back in the morning, Redman thought helplessly. Keep himself alive, and keep Jennifer alive, while they were hunted down in the dark by men with machine-guns.

Using extreme caution, he looked over the top of the boulder, straining his eyes in the dusk to see how much time he had. There was no movement on the airstrip, but he fancied he could pick out figures over on the north boundary by the mangroves.

Twenty, perhaps thirty seconds, Redman decided. Then the bastards would be on top of him.

Kneeling down, he unbuttoned Jennifer's jacket. There were holes in it, and it was saturated in blood.

Her eyes flickered for a second.

'Jennifer,' he whispered. 'Can you hear me?'

When she didn't answer, he peeled back the jacket. She had been shot in the back three times. Two of the bullets had made their exit through her left breast. The third had punctured her stomach.

'Oh, Jesus,' he breathed. 'Jennifer talk to me. For Christ's sake talk to me.'

She began to say something, but choked on a rush of bright red blood.

Knowing he dare not move her, and aware that each second he stayed reduced his own chances of survival, Redman started counting under his breath.

Sixteen seconds after he'd begun, Jennifer Decker died cradled in his arms.

He kissed her once on the lips, gently closed her eyes, then slithered out from behind the rock and began crawling away into the shadows of the jungle.

Three

Taking his feet off the coffee table, Owen Mitchell peered through his glasses as though they had become suddenly opaque.

'Jesus bloody Christ,' he said.

So far, apparently content to leave his questions for later, he had been quiet, listening to Redman's summary of what had happened over the last five days without showing much interest. Only now, after hearing a watered-down description of the horror at the airstrip, did Owen appear to have grasped the implication of what Redman had been trying to explain.

Redman himself was having trouble with the explanation. On the return flight to Brisbane he'd rehearsed this a hundred times, but presenting a coherent account of something he wanted to forget was proving more difficult than he expected. Worse still, reliving the events had brought back the reality of what had happened, and he could feel the anger welling up inside him again.

'How the hell did you get away?' Owen took off his glasses and started polishing them.

'God knows,' Redman said. 'It was a nightmare. I just kept going up the river until I couldn't go any further. All

I remember is coming across a bloody great wall of rock and trying to climb the damn thing in the dark.'

'Did the guys off the launch follow you?'

'They may have done. I don't know. I couldn't hear anything over the noise of the river. My guess is that they tried, but decided it was too difficult.'

'So you spent the night on the rock wall.'

Redman nodded. 'About fifty feet up. I stayed on a ledge until Jimmy came back in the morning. He had a couple of Malaitan islanders with him. They went to see if the launch was still there, but there was no sign of it. Jimmy reckoned we were lucky the *Kwaibala* hadn't gone too.'

'Well, you're a lucky bastard all round then, aren't you? What did the police say?'

Redman was silent.

'You did report it?'

'No,' Redman said shortly. 'Jimmy figured it was too much of a mess to explain to anyone. I thought I'd do something about it when I got back here – after I've sorted out things better.'

'Well, that's real smart. My friend, you are heading into deep shit. You know that, don't you?' Owen frowned. 'What about Jennifer?'

'As soon as we left on the boat, the Malaitans took her body up into the hills – back to their village.' Redman paused. 'Look, you haven't had time to put all this together – I have – or some of it, anyway. No matter how nasty things were over there, I can't see any sense in giving the police some half-baked story they're not going to believe. No one believed Jennifer Decker. People thought she was crazy.'

'No one was dead then.'

'Yes they were,' Redman said. 'You've forgotten her husband. Jennifer was killed because she was trying to find out how he died. I was damn nearly killed for the same reason. Whoever was flying those crop dusters off the airstrip aren't playing games. They're making sure no one interferes with them. That's why they were watching Jennifer's home – why they searched my room at the hotel.'

'Who's they?'

'The people with the launch – the tall guy – whoever was on the squid boat. I don't know.'

'So you plan to go to the police here in Australia. When you have it all nicely figured out.' Owen's voice was caustic. 'Someone's been shot, murdered for Christ's sake.'

'Owen,' Redman said. 'Just shut up, will you. I'm here for some help not a goddamn lecture. You never met Jennifer Decker, you haven't been to the Solomon Islands, and in the last two days, no one's tried to kill you with a machine-gun.'

'Did you come straight from the airport?' Owen went to a cupboard. 'How about a drink?'

'Yes, I came straight from the airport, and yes, please, I'd like a drink.'

Owen half filled two glasses with bourbon. He pointed to some folders and a stack of books on top of the cupboard. 'See those?'

'Books on dust?'

'Dust explosions. After you called me from Honiara I did some reading.' He returned to the table, giving Redman one of the glasses. 'You have no idea what you've got yourself into.'

Redman used the alcohol to make himself relax, feeling the warmth of it spread through him with the first mouthful. He drank more, being careful to keep his mind focused on the present. The trick had worked before, he remembered, the same trick he'd used for Josie. Concentrate on today, or tomorrow, or next week. Never think about yesterday, and never imagine the past could ever have been different.

'Can you make dust explode?' he asked.

Owen nodded. 'You want a child's guide?'

'Sure.'

'I'll get my notes.' Owen went to collect the bottle and one of his folders.

Before he sat down again, he squinted at Redman. 'Are you sure you want to do this?' he said. 'You look terrible.'

'I'm sure.' Redman swallowed more bourbon, watching Owen shuffle paper around on the table.

His hands were no larger than Jennifer's, Redman thought. In fact, Owen himself was no larger. It was only because of his personality, or perhaps simply because he was so extraordinarily clever, that people gained the impression that he was of a normal size. No one seemed to notice the thick glasses, his skinny arms and his pale complexion. Nor were they ever offended by Owen's use of the most unsavoury language at the most inopportune time – not even women who were attracted to him as though he was irresistible.

Redman had known Owen for nearly two years, but still occasionally forgot that he was not like anyone else.

'Right.' Owen was ready to begin. 'It goes like this. Historical perspective. The first recorded dust exploison happened in 1785. In an Italian flour mill.'

'Flour,' Redman said. 'Flour dust?'

'Yes. The kind of material doesn't matter much. If it's dry and it burns, and you can make it into dust, you can make it explode. It depends on the size of the particles, the concentration of them and what trigger you use to set off the explosion. If you try hard enough, you can get a bang from nearly anything.' Owen smiled. 'Not that anyone ever tries. Dust explosions are accidents – industrial accidents mostly.'

'Fatal accidents,' Redman said.

'Right. It was explosions in coal mines that made people start worrying about dust. In the 1800s there were mine disasters all the time, all over the world. Everyone thought they were caused by a build-up of underground gas seeping into the mine shafts. They were partly right. Usually it was methane gas that started the explosions. What people didn't realize then, is that a small gas explosion stirs up all the coal dust that's lying around.

'About the turn of the century, after there were some bloody enormous explosions in English and French coal mines, scientists finally figured out that dust was the real problem.'

'Will coal dust explode by itself?' Redman drained his glass. 'Without being stirred up by burning gas?'

'You bet. So will cotton seed, soy flour, cocoa, wood dust, coffee, most of the plastics, charcoal and some metals. I've told you – anything that'll burn. Some dusts make a bigger bang than others, but they're all as dangerous as hell.'

'How dangerous?'

'I'll come to that. Don't rush me. Do you want more history?'

'Not for the minute.' Redman held out his glass for a refill. 'So what happens if you're not in a building or in an underground coal mine? Suppose you're out in the middle of the Pacific Ocean.'

'Ah.' Owen had been waiting for the question. 'That's the clever bit. The research data says three things are necessary for an explosion to occur. A combustible dust contained in something like a room or a mine shaft; the right concentration of dust, and an ignition source. That's straightforward, isn't it?'

'Sure.' Redman was growing impatient. 'But I don't want to know about lab tests. Tell me what would happen to a cloud of dust floating in the air over the ocean.'

'I am telling you. Just listen. Obviously, if you're out in the Pacific, there isn't any containment – no walls, no floor and no roof. It's not like a coal mine or a steel flask in a laboratory.'

'So?'

'So, in theory, you can't generate a dust explosion.'

Owen paused for effect. 'Not unless it's a big, motherfucker of an explosion.'

'I don't understand.'

'If you do it right, if you set out to make a real big bang, you don't need to contain the dust inside anything. Once the burning velocity reaches the speed of sound, the air around the fireball can't move out of the way fast enough to relieve the pressure. So the surrounding air acts like a solid wall – or a floor or a ceiling.' He removed his glasses. 'Then things get exciting.'

Redman stood up and walked over to the window. Outside, the evening rush hour had begun. Traffic was backing up at the end of the road as Brisbane commuters started their fight to get on to the Pacific Highway for the journey south, and there was a fog of exhaust fumes hanging over the city.

He felt strangely numb, unwilling to ask more questions because the answers were making the puzzle more complicated than he wanted it to be.

Owen came over to the window. He was holding a book. 'Listen,' he said. 'Tennessee, USA. January 1993. A bulldozer was being loaded from an outdoor pile of burnt slag, fifty feet high. The pile was free-standing, with only a low wall at the back of it. A major slide threw a large volume of dust into the air which was accidentally ignited by a piece of glowing coal. The explosion killed fifty-eight people in a nearby factory, and destroyed the bulldozer completely. Parts of it were found half a mile away. They didn't even look for the driver. That's a typical unconfined dust explosion. A little one.'

Redman continued staring out the window.

Owen leafed through the book. 'There's something else in here, too,' he said. 'Immediately after Hiroshima – for the first few hours after the Americans had dropped the bomb – the Japanese had no idea what had hit them. All they knew was what they'd seen with their own eyes. So they made a guess – their scientists did.'

'Don't tell me,' Redman said slowly. 'They believed it was a dust explosion.'

'Exactly. They thought American planes had dropped magnesium powder over part of the city. The Japanese figured it had drifted down in a cloud until it hit the power lines. Those scientists were pretty smart people – even though they were wrong.'

'I'm not sure any of this is going to help,' Redman said. 'I told Jennifer Decker she might never sort out what happened to her husband.'

'You know damn well what happened to him. The poor bastard flew into a cloud of explosive dust. His plane probably triggered the explosion to start with.'

'That's too easy. I've already explained. Crop-dusting aircraft couldn't carry dust that far out to sea from the airstrip. Anyway, that's not what I meant. I meant we're never going to know why someone wanted to set off a bloody great explosion way out in the South Pacific.'

'Explosions plural,' Owen said. 'You told me the fishermen saw two – two flashes of lightning on different days. They said the first one wasn't too far offshore.'

'So what? It doesn't explain what's been going on.' Redman stuck his hands in his pockets. 'Unless the Americans or a group of mad terrorists have been developing some kind of new bomb in the Solomon Islands.'

'They'd have to be bloody stupid, wouldn't they?' Owen snorted. 'No one's that brainless. A dust bomb would be the most strategically useless idea anyone could think of. Imagine it, a bunch of little crop dusters flying backwards and forwards over Baghdad through heavy anti-aircraft fire at the tremendous speed of fifty miles an hour, or however fast they go. Then it rains so the dust gets wet. Then a wind starts up and ninety percent of the dust is blown away before you can ignite it. Great weapon system.'

'What's your explanation, then?' Redman said.

'I haven't got one. But you can forget bombs. Modern weapons have two fundamental components, a nuclear or high-explosive warhead and a means of delivering the warhead to the target. If you can't deliver, you haven't got a weapon system.'

'OK, OK.' Redman's impatience had returned. 'So what do I do? Forget what's happened? Write a report for Airtech saying Warren Decker's plane just disappeared and his wife fell of a cliff?'

'Take it one step at a time. Did you bring back some of the dust?'

Redman walked across to his suitcase, lifted the lid and rummaged around inside. Then he started transferring spent machine-gun cartridges and other bits and pieces to the coffee table. When he'd finished, there was a row of exhibits for Owen to examine.

'Those are the dust samples.' Redman pointed to two manila envelopes. 'Dust from the airstrip in one, dust from the seat squab in the other. Jimmy and I had to break into Jennifer's home to get the squab sample. The envelopes are marked so you can't get them mixed up.'

Owen picked up the pair of detonators. 'I know what these little bastards are,' he said. 'Bet you they were used with dynamite to trigger the dust.'

'But you don't know what this is, do you?' Redman handed him an elaborately carved figure of a human head. It was highly polished and made from an extremely dark, dense wood. 'It's a *nguzunguzu.*'

'What do you do with it?'

'Nothing, unless you have a canoe to put it on. It's a Solomon Island spirit – for good luck. Jimmy gave it to me.'

'Does it work?'

Redman grinned. 'Maybe.' He was feeling better. The episode on Malaita was less vivid in his mind than it had been earlier, and here, in Owen's apartment, close to the bustling heart of Brisbane, it was possible to believe the airstrip was a place that existed only in his imagination.

Except that it did exist, he thought. The carved figure of the *nguzunguzu* was no more part of his imagination than Jennifer's camera lying on the table in front of him.

He picked up the camera and opened the back of it.

'Mrs Decker's, I presume,' Owen said.

'I found it on the runway. She must have dropped it when we were running.' Redman removed the film and tossed the canister to Owen. 'Can you develop that at the university? I don't want to take it to an ordinary processing lab.'

'Why don't you?'

'Because there is a photograph of Jennifer on it.' Redman paused. 'I took it the next morning – afterwards.'

Owen raised his eyebrows.

'I just took it, OK.'

'Fine.' Owen knew better than to comment. 'What's that?' He pointed to a crumpled packet of foil.

'Anti-malaria pills. I only unpacked them to remind myself to take one. Jennifer said I should carry on with them for a few days when I got back.'

'You liked her, didn't you?'

'Not in the way you mean.' Redman used his fingernail to pop out a chloroquine tablet.

'Take that after dinner. Come on, you can help me fix some spaghetti. Then you can bunk down in my spare room.'

'I'll go home, thanks.' Redman stretched. 'As long as you'll give me a lift. We'll finish your bourbon first, though.'

Finishing the bourbon was a mistake. After living on his nerves for the last forty-eight hours, Redman was in no condition for drinking. At ten o'clock when he left the apartment his eyes were drooping, and no sooner was he inside the car than he fell asleep.

When he came to, Owen was shaking him by the shoulder.

'Are you awake?' Owen continued with the shaking.

'Yes, leave off, will you.' Redman climbed out of the car, going to retrieve his case from the trunk before coming back to say goodbye.

'You sure you're all right?' Owen said.

'I'm fine. Thanks for dinner. I'll call you tomorrow.'

'Don't bother. I'll be at the university all day. I'll give you a ring when I get home.' Owen gunned the engine. 'For Christ's sake go and get some sleep.'

When the car had gone, Redman started off across the road, only to be intercepted by a young woman who appeared from nowhere.

'I wouldn't if I were you,' she said.

He put down his case. 'I beg your pardon?'

'That's your house, isn't it? You are Steve Redman?'

In the dark it was hard to see her face properly, but as far as he could make out, he'd never met her before. She had blonde hair pulled back into a pony-tail, and she was wearing some sort of tailored trouser suit. She was also wearing high-heeled shoes.

'Do we know each other?' Redman said politely.

She laughed. 'I'm sorry. My name's Debbie Hinton.' She gave him a card. 'I work for WPA.'

'That's nice.' He had no idea what WPA might be. 'If you were me, what wouldn't you do?'

'I wouldn't go into your house – not right away.' Without being asked, she picked up his case and carried it back to the sidewalk.

Redman followed her, more awake than he had been a moment ago.

Opening her handbag, she took out a newspaper, holding it up for him to see in the light from a neighbouring house. An article at the bottom of the page was headed WIFE OF MISSING PILOT SLAMS US AIRCRAFT MANUFACTURER.

'Are you a journalist?' he asked.

'WPA. World Press Agency. I didn't write this article, though. The competition got the story first. My boss saw it and said I ought to come to Brisbane and see if I could interview you.' She returned the paper to her handbag. 'Your office told me you were due back from the Solomons two days ago, but when you didn't show up, I telephoned your hotel in Honiara and then started calling you at home. Today I decided to come here in case you were deliberately trying to avoid seeing anyone.' She paused. 'The only way to do a job like mine is to try everything you can think of. You always have to keep trying.'

'Have you finished?' Redman said.

'Mm.' She nodded. 'I thought you'd want me to explain.'

'I do. What's this about my house?'

'I've been here all evening. In my car.' She pointed to a red Toyota parked along the street. 'About an hour and a half ago, three men arrived in a BMW. After two of them had fiddled around to unlock your front door they took a parcel inside. When they came out again they didn't have it anymore.' She smiled brightly. 'It's probably nothing.'

'And the third man?' Redman queried.

'He stayed outside with a hand-held radio. I could see him talking into it from my car. Have you got friends with a BMW? It was a dark-green one.'

'No.' He was finding it hard to believe what she was saying.

'You don't look too well,' she said. 'If you don't mind me saying so.'

'I'm tired.'

'Is your house insured?'

Redman looked at her. 'It's rented. By Airtech – the company I work for.'

'That's good.' She opened her handbag again, this time taking out a ball of string. 'I bought this at the store on the corner before it closed, in case you turned up. I left a note telling you not to do anything before I got back.' She held out her hand. 'Let me have your front door key.'

Redman gave it to her. 'Are you sure you're a journalist?' he said.

'I am, really. It's just that I happen to have worked for sixteen months in Lebanon – in 1990.' She started lashing the head of the key to one end of a pencil to form an L. 'Does your door open inwards?'

He nodded.

'We'll need the spare wheel from my car, then.'

He accompanied her to the Toyota where he removed the spare from the trunk while she finished working on the key. By now, the situation had become sufficiently unreal for Redman to have given up wondering why he was walking up and down the street in the dark with a girl he didn't know. She had assumed control in a matter-of-fact way, as though there was nothing unusual about what she was doing, as though she was operating in some terrorist-ridden city instead of deepest suburban Brisbane.

'Roll the wheel along,' she instructed. 'We have to lean it against your door.'

She trotted along beside him on her heels, unravelling her ball of string as she went, until they were again outside Redman's house.

Gingerly he inclined the wheel, resting the top of the tyre against the door. When he straightened up, he saw she had already inserted the key in the lock and was in the process of threading the string through a bolt hole in the wheel. He understood now. The pencil was a lever. By attaching the string to the end of it she would be able to unlock the door from a safe distance. After that, the wheel would take over, forcing the door open by its own weight. It was fairly ingenious, Redman thought, mainly because it was so simple.

She was attempting to fasten the string to the pencil, but fumbling because her hands were shaking.

'Here, let me do it.' He slipped a clove hitch over the pencil and pulled the knot tight.

'I had these friends in Beirut,' she said. 'They used to open their door like this whenever they'd been out of town.'

Redman tried unsuccessfully to see her face in the lights of a passing car. 'This is crazy,' he said. 'You know that, don't you?'

'I know if someone had left a surprise parcel for me in my house I'd be pleased. I wouldn't be suspicious. Your trip to the Solomons must have been quite interesting.'

'Journalists make me suspicious,' Redman said. 'Fast-talking lady journalists.'

Collecting his suitcase from the sidewalk, he headed off along the street, letting the string slide through his fingers until he reached her car.

When she caught up with him, she was out of breath.

'Do I get an interview?' she asked.

He leaned into the Toyota, switching on the interior lights so he could see her better. She was rather pretty, with large eyes and a mouth which was set in a half smile, either because she was amused or because she was mocking him for some reason.

'Do you figure I owe you an interview?' he said.

'Find out.'

Winding the string round his hand Redman gently began to pull. He felt the line tighten and then suddenly go slack.

He had almost decided nothing was going to happen when there was a sharp crack followed by an earsplitting bang.

Twenty-five yards away, part of his front door sailed out into the street on a wave of flame. Slivers of broken glass and pieces of smouldering timber rained down in neighbouring gardens through a haze of acrid-smelling smoke.

In the other houses, lights were coming on. People were shouting and beginning to appear at windows.

Redman had been unprepared for the violence of the

blast. He had expected nothing like this. It was the machine-gun at the airstrip all over again – deliberate, cold-blooded overkill to compensate for any errors. But again there had been a miscalculation, and again he had escaped – this time because of a girl with big eyes and a pony tail – a complete stranger whom he had known for less than thirty minutes.

'Is there somewhere else you can go?' she asked. 'I can give you a lift if you like. Or do you want to wait for the police?'

It was her way of warning him, he realized. And just as he knew he was in no position to stay here she knew what his answer would be.

She opened the car door for him.

It was not until the Toyota reached the end of the street that he thought to give her directions to Owen's apartment, and only then did he remember to slip a hand into his pocket to touch the carved wooden head of the *nguzunguzu*.

Four

Afternoon sunshine was making the apartment uncomfortably warm. The stuffiness was giving Redman a headache, and the rattle from Owen's air-conditioning unit was getting on his nerves.

He went over to thump it with his fist.

'Turn if off.' Debbie Hinton closed her notebook. 'I don't think it's working anyway.'

He pulled out the plug before returning to his chair.

'I've been sitting down too long,' he said. 'I need some fresh air.'

'Is it all right if I ask you a few more questions? Or do you want to go out?'

'I can't go out. Hawthorne's supposed to be calling me.' Redman inspected his watch. 'His secretary said he'd be back in his office at three o'clock, our time.'

'I'll make some coffee.' She stood up. 'Your friend won't mind me poking around in his kitchen, will he?'

'Owen doesn't mind anything. There's instant coffee in the cupboard over the sink.' Redman watched her walk across the room.

Ever since last night he'd been wondering what she really looked like. At midday, when she'd arrived for her appointment, he had found out. As a result, he had spent much of the afternoon trying to analyse why he found her so extraordinarily attractive. Apart from her eyes and her rather elegant slender legs, there was nothing particularly unusual about her, yet within minutes of her being in the room, he'd become aware of her in a way which was continuing to unsettle him.

Today she was wearing a sleeveless blouse and a short, wine-coloured skirt. A ribbon of the same colour held back her hair in a long pony-tail extending half-way down her back. On and off, over the last hour, Redman had been imagining what she would look like with the ribbon untied and her hair loose around her shoulders. The thought had irritated him to the point where he had forced himself to stop watching her altogether. It had not, however, prevented him from continuing to wonder what it was that drew his eyes to her wherever she went.

He could see her now, busy in the kitchen.

'Sugar?' she called out.

'One spoon.' He directed his attention elsewhere, tidying up the books on dust explosions he'd been reading earlier today. Two of the books contained information he could understand, but the remainder were either incomprehensible to him or dealt exclusively with coal mines.

'Are they Owen's?' Debbie carried a tray into the room.

Redman nodded. 'Owen reads books like other people read newspapers. Give him a couple more days and he'll be a world expert on dust explosions.'

She smiled. 'Knowing about them won't explain what happened to you in the Solomons.'

'It's a start. If Owen can't figure this out, no one can. Anyway, I trust him. This isn't exactly something I can talk about to people I don't know.'

'Like me, you mean?'

'You didn't give me much choice,' Redman said. 'All I'm trying to do is stop you writing some half-cocked story that'll make things more difficult.'

'Do you trust your boss? Why did you try to call him this morning?'

'Because if I wait until after the weekend, he'll start worrying,' he said. 'He might be able to help, too.'

'I can help you more than he can.'

'I haven't asked you,' Redman said. 'I might decide to leave the whole damn thing alone.'

'No, you won't. You wouldn't have spent the last three hours telling me the weirdest story I've ever heard if you weren't going ahead with it. You have to go on with it.'

'So you can get an exclusive.'

She smoothed down her skirt. 'You said I could have the story as long as I promised not to write anything until you have it wrapped up. I can help you do that. Does it matter why I want to help?'

'No, I guess not.' He grinned. 'You don't have to be all prickly about it, though.

'I'm not prickly. You don't understand. I'm only a junior reporter at WPA. Juniors don't often get good assignments. I don't want to let this one get away.'

'How long have you been working for WPA?' he asked.

'Just over three years. I'm supposed to be based in London, but I go all over the place. I've been here in Australia since mid-April – working out of WPA's Sydney office.'

'Are you English?' Redman had been endeavouring to pick her accent.

'No. I went to school in England but I was born in Canada. My father's Canadian. My mother was Jewish.'

He drank some coffee, wondering whether the complexion of her skin came from her mother or whether she was tanned from being out in the sun.

'What about the other questions?' he said. 'We might as well get them over with.'

'Oh.' She reopened her notebook. 'Well, first off, I don't understand about the crop dusters. If you're right about Warren Decker's plane igniting a dust cloud in the

Solomons, how come the crop dusters don't blow themselves up when they're dropping tons of dust all over the place?'

'They don't just drop it,' Redman said. 'Not in one hit. It's released from under the fuselage at a fixed rate, so it can be spread over a large area. The dust streams out behind in a plume. If you flew half-a-dozen dusters alongside each other at the same altitude it would be absolutely safe.'

'Their engines won't suck in dust because it's dispersed behind the planes. Is that right?'

'Right. They may have special filters fitted to their air-intakes, too. I don't know.'

'But there weren't half-a-dozen planes flying off the airstrip, were there?' she frowned.

'The Malaitans saw at least two. They weren't sure how many there were.'

'Mm. And you think they were American-built planes.'

'It's a guess,' Redman said. 'There aren't that many companies manufacturing crop dusters. From the islanders' description of them I think there's a chance they were AT 302s. They're made by Rockwell.'

She scribbled in her notebook. 'If they are AT 302s, can you find out who's been buying them?'

He nodded. 'If they've been bought recently, I can. That's what I want to ask Hawthorne. Market intelligence in the aircraft business is pretty good nowadays.'

'Now tell me about the squid boat – the name of it. You said one of the islanders saw some letters on the hull, but they'd been painted over. What were they?'

'I think it was the complete name,' Redman said. 'The old guy in the canoe wasn't sure but he didn't speak English, let alone Chinese. Jimmy and I spent a lot of time trying to figure it out. If we're right, the boat was called the *Zhongshai*.'

'OK.' She picked up her coffee cup. 'I'll see if my office can find out where it was registered. I only have a couple more questions – do you mind?'

'Go ahead.' Redman was looking at her ankles.

'This tall man from the launch, can you describe him to me?'

'Why?'

'I just thought it'd be handy to know.'

'Over six feet,' Redman said. 'Dark, wavy hair, high cheek-bones, moustache. How's that?'

'European?'

'I'm not certain. He wasn't an Asian. He might have had brown eyes. I can't remember.'

Her next question was interrupted by the telephone.

Placing a finger on his lips to indicate she should be quiet, Redman picked up the receiver. It was Hawthorne.

'Thought I'd better touch base,' Redman said.

'Where the hell are you?' Hawthorne's voice was clipped. 'I've been trying to call you at home but your phone doesn't work. When I called your office yesterday, Trixie said she didn't know where you were. Why doesn't your secretary know what's going on?'

'I'm at a friend's place. I haven't been to the office yet.'

'So what happened in the Solomon Islands? What did you find out?'

'Not a lot,' Redman said cautiously.

'Doesn't sound like it. I've got an avalanche of faxes here – all from that goddamn Australian newspaper – the *Queensland Tribune*. They say they can't get hold of the Decker woman and they want to know where you are.' Hawthorne paused. 'Whatever you've been doing, you've stirred up a lot of shit. I've had someone from Washington round here asking questions.'

In Redman's head, the warning bells were suddenly much louder. 'Who?' he said.

'A smart-arse from the Federal Aviation Authority – a Colonel Lawrence Corliss.'

'What's this got to do with the FAA?' Redman asked.

'Corliss wanted to know whether our aircraft are certified for airworthiness in the States before we ship them overseas. I told him it was a stupid question. That's when he got all official. Anyway, he wants to talk to you. He'll be phoning your office. If he starts on about certification for Decker's Eagle, tell him to look in his own files.'

'OK.' Redman was uneasy. 'I need some information,' he said. 'For the Indonesian order.'

'Like what?'

'Do you have the phone number of those market research people in San Jose? They're called Aviation International or something. We used them last year, remember?'

'Yeah, hang on.' Hawthorne read out a number. 'You haven't told me what happened to Decker's plane. What's the story?'

'He was off course,' Redman said. 'And low on fuel. A couple of local fishermen think they saw him ditch, but they didn't find anything.'

'You writing it up as navigational error?'

'Pilot error,' Redman said. 'We don't want this colonel thinking there was something wrong with the instruments, do we?'

'No,' Hawthorne grunted. 'When are you going to fax your report?'

'After I've sent off the Indonesian quote. I'm a bit behind. I'll get Trixie to type it on Monday.'

'You're not in any trouble, are you Steve? The Decker woman didn't give you a hard time?'

Redman swore under his breath. 'No, I'm fine. I'll be in touch.' He rang off, wondering what on earth had prompted Hawthorne to ask the question.

Debbie had been listening. She came over to him. 'Is everything all right?' she asked.

This was the closest he'd been to her today, close enough for him to smell her perfume and see a tiny scar or blemish at the corner of her mouth.

'I'll tell you later,' he said. 'Let's get some air.'

'Shall I drive you somewhere? It's not far to the beach from here.'

'You haven't got a spare wheel.' Redman smiled. 'And I'm not sure it's a good idea for me to go home and get my car – not anymore.'

She raised her eyebrows.

'How about a walk?'

'All right.' Briefly her eyes met his. 'Walking would be nice.'

Over the course of the weekend, Redman was to do a good deal of walking with Debbie Hinton. It proved to be a way for him to come to terms with the events of the last week, and refine his thoughts about a girl who's company he enjoyed more on each occasion he met her.

For two days they talked, sometimes with Owen, sometimes by themselves, exploring explanations for the dust explosions, discussing possible reasons for the bomb and reconsidering Redman's options. But by Sunday night, despite feeling more alive than he had done for months, he had reached no conclusions.

Information from California on the crop dusters had led nowhere, and the mystery of the dust explosions remained unsolved. Nor had he made any progress towards determining whether or not he should contact the police or seek help from another source.

Redman was certain of only two things: the longer he did nothing, the greater the danger would become, and that his resolve to solve the puzzle was now much stronger. He was not concerned about the danger. Instead, because his life had been turned upside down, he was conscious of a new-found willingness to go forwards again. And with it, almost overriding his fascination with Debbie, had come something more important – the realization that he was, at last, on the verge of accepting Josie's death.

He spent Monday morning alone, beginning to worry

about the lack of fresh information, knowing that unless they made a breakthrough in the next few days, the trail would soon become too cold to follow.

The breakthrough occurred at four o'clock. Preceding it by a few minutes came the bad news.

Shortly after Debbie had telephoned to say she was on her way, Owen stormed into the apartment, throwing a copy of the evening newspaper at Redman as soon as he was inside the door.

'*Tribune*,' Owen said. 'Page three. If you thought the shit wasn't going to hit the fan, you were dead bloody wrong.'

Redman found page three and had just begun to read when Debbie arrived. She was evidently pleased about something.

'Hi.' She smiled at Owen. 'You said you wouldn't be home before six.'

'I hadn't read the newspaper, then. Have you seen it?'

'No.' She glanced at Redman. 'Why? What's happened?'

'Listen.' He started at the beginning again, reading the article out loud.

'Solomon Island authorities are treating the disappearance of Mrs Jennifer Decker as serious. Mrs Decker is the wife of Australian-born Warren Decker, missing since his aircraft failed to arrive at Auki on the island of Malaita following an unscheduled flight from San Cristobal on March 10th this year.

Honiara police report that Mrs Decker was last seen in the company of Steven Redman, a representative from Airtech a US company best known for its manufacture of the single-engined Airtech Eagle – the aircraft employed by Mr Decker for his inter-island business flights.

Airtech in California are uncertain of Redman's whereabouts at present. They deny that Redman was sent to the Solomon Islands to prevent Mrs Decker from continuing to claim her husband's aircraft was unsafe.

Local police have so far been unable to contact the

Brisbane-based Airtech representative since his return to Australia. They are anxious to do so, particularly after an unexplained fire at Redman's $300,000 rented townhouse late on Friday night.'

'You'd have to be brain-dead not to get the message, wouldn't you?' Owen said. 'Steven Redman flies to Honiara; gets rid of Jennifer Decker to shut her up; flies back to Brisbane, then disappears after destroying incriminating evidence by blowing up his own home.'

'That's not what it says.' Debbie took the paper and started to read it herself.

'Yes, it is.' Redman had been expecting something like this all along. 'You're a journalist,' he said. 'You'd have written it the same way.'

She didn't answer him.

He put his hands on her shoulders. 'Never mind the damn newspaper. Forget it. What were you so cheerful about five minutes ago?'

'I know who killed Jennifer Decker, who planted the bomb.' She carefully removed his hands. 'I know who's behind the dust explosions – the whole thing.'

'Libya?' Redman said. 'Or the Vatican?'

'I'm serious. WPA faxed me last night from London. I've been on the telephone all morning – following up details. I can tell you who organized the explosions in the Solomons.'

'Who?' He still didn't believe her.

'A company called Consolidated Metals. It's a British company from Birmingham in England. WPA did a computer search of all the international shipping registers. Then they cross-checked with marine insurance underwriters in New York. They found a boat called the *Zhongshan*. You and Jimmy had the right name except for the last letter. There isn't one called the *Zhongshai*.'

'Go on,' Redman said.

'The *Zhongshan* was Taiwanese owned but registered in

Hong Kong. Ten months ago it was sold for scrap to a Hong Kong company called International Metal Traders – IMT.'

'And IMT are a subsidiary of Consolidated Metals.' Owen interrupted. 'Right?'

Debbie nodded. 'Consolidated Metals own companies all over the world, mostly in British Commonwealth countries.' She glanced at Redman. 'When you phoned that California market research company on Friday, they said Rockwell had delivered nine AT 302 crop dusters to a company in India, didn't they?'

'Patna Aviation,' Redman said. 'This time last year.'

'Guess who owns Patna Aviation?'

'Jesus.' He was astonished.

'I haven't finished. Another fax came in from WPA at lunchtime today. It's a breakdown of Consolidated Metals' holdings worldwide, listing the business activities of each company.' Debbie paused. 'There's an Australian division of IMT in Brisbane – an address in Normanby. That's where I've been. I went there this afternoon.'

'Oh smart move,' Owen said. 'What did you do? Flash your tits at the manager and ask if he'd shot anyone lately.'

Debbie had already learned how to handle Owen. She smiled sweetly at him. 'I just wanted to have a look. It's one of those shared office complexes where they have a couple of typist secretaries and a telephone operator who work for half-a-dozen different companies – small companies who can't afford their own full-time staff. Anyway, it was a waste of time. IMT closed down their office last Thursday. It's empty.'

Redman sat down on a bar stool, unable to decide whether the new pieces were helping solve the puzzle or whether it had just become twice as big as it was before.

'OK,' he said. 'So a British company uses its overseas subsidiaries to buy the squid boat and the crop dusters. The same company has been operating in Australia.

Where does that get us? It doesn't tell us why Consolidated Metals or International Metal Traders have been experimenting with dust explosions in the Solomon Islands. It doesn't tell us anything.'

'Yes, it does,' Owen said. 'You've answered your own question. Experimenting is exactly what they've been doing – experimenting – in secret. If you wanted to make some really big bangs without anyone knowing, where would you go? Where can you find a disused airstrip that gives you access to one of the most remote parts of the Pacific?' He stopped for a moment. 'Cloudy days,' he said. 'Shit, I should've thought of it before.'

'What?' Redman had lost the thread of the argument.

'Both explosions were on cloudy days. There's less chance of flashes being picked up by a satellite if you have cloud cover. IMT are being tricky. They've been testing something so secret they don't even want the Americans to know about it.'

Debbie shook her head. 'You're making it sound as though they've been testing a bomb. We know that's not true. You said using dust to make a bomb would be crazy.'

'So IMT were playing around with something else. Don't rush it. We're getting there.' Owen took a sheet of paper out of his brief-case. 'My news isn't as interesting,' he said. 'But it gives us a fix on the dust. I got the preliminary results from the lab analysis today. The silver material is high-purity aluminium. It's been made into flakes – very tiny flakes, beween ten and twenty microns across. That's about half the diameter of a gnat's cock.' He grinned at Debbie. 'A small gnat with a hard on. The black dust is coal – or what's left of it – mostly charred residue. The particles have been burned up in the explosion – by the heat from the flame front.'

'Aren't the aluminium flakes burnt too?' Redman asked.

'Not all of them. Some are only partly oxidized or

they're recondensed, unreacted flakes.' Owen looked up. 'Coal dust ignites at a temperature of 300 degrees Fahrenheit – that's fairly low. For ten-micron aluminium flake you need over twice that temperature. Our clever British friends used the coal dust to create a fireball that was hot enough to set off the aluminium. That made it real dangerous – a nasty two-stage bastard.'

'So why aren't all the aluminium flakes burnt?' Redman asked.

'I won't know that until I get the rest of the lab results, but probably because there was a higher concentration of them in the mixture. It doesn't matter a hell of a lot if some of the dust settles out in the atmosphere before you trigger the explosion. IMT didn't care how much aluminium dust they wasted. They still got bigger bangs for their money than they'd get from anything else – a lot bigger.'

'More than from a nuclear warhead?' Debbie asked.

'Depends on how much dust you want to scatter around. These guys aren't thinking small, though. This is big-scale stuff.'

'Nuclear scale?' Debbie was insistent. She stood in front of him waiting for an answer.

'Sure.' Owen studied her carefully, letting his eyes rest on her blouse. 'Except a dust explosion is nice and clean. No fall-out, zero radioactivity. Just a great big fucking bang.'

She smiled at him again. 'All noise and hot air. A bit like you, Owen, don't you think?'

Redman was amused. Ever since Owen had realized his technique was failing, he had adopted a different approach to Debbie. But, as usual, in this exchange he had again lost ground, disarmed by her tactic of being artificially charming whenever he tried to intimidate her.

Owen was unperturbed. He took some photographs from his brief-case and handed them to Redman.

'Jennifer's film?'

Owen nodded, watching while Redman spread them out in a row on the bench-top.

They were all there. Pictures of Jimmy at the wheel of the *Kwaibala*, shots of gas cylinders, empty drums and rubbish inside the hut at the airstrip, wheel marks on the runway, the mangroves, the river, and finally, the photographs Redman himself had taken. It showed Jennifer lying dead behind the boulder in a pool of blood.

Debbie turned her face away. 'Who in the name of God would ever do something like that?' she said quietly.

'Consolidated Metals,' Redman said. 'Or International Metal Traders. The same people who planted the bomb in my home.'

'Well I think we ought to pay a visit to IMT's office.' She gathered up the photos, putting them to one side. 'It's only one room on the ground floor.'

'Why?' Redman was surprised by the suggestion.

'I don't know. To see if they left anything behind. They only moved out on Thursday. That's less than three days ago.'

'Break in, you mean?'

'We might not have to. If the building has contract cleaners they'll let us in. It's not as if we want to burgle one of the other companies there.'

'You wouldn't be trying to pretend you've just thought of this, would you?' Redman said.

'Part of the training. First law of journalism. Always keep one step ahead of everyone else.'

'And always keep trying.'

'Mm. We could go now – this evening. I gave WPA the phone number here – in case they have more information – but if Owen doesn't mind staying behind, he can take the call.'

'We'll have to go in your car,' Redman said.

She nodded. 'I bought a new spare wheel today. You owe me three hundred and ten dollars.'

'I'll buy you dinner,' he said. 'On the way back.

Anywhere you like.'

It was gone nine when they arrived at the Normanby office complex a featureless, glass-fronted building in a street running parallel with the Bulimba to Ipswich railroad.

Venetian blinds covering the windows made it difficult for Redman to see inside, but as far as he could make out, all the offices were in darkness.

'Where shall I park?' Debbie slowed the car.

'Anywhere.'

She let the Toyota coast to a halt near a large illuminated sign.

He read out the names on it. 'Imported Ceramics, Pacific Printers, Doctor Chu Nan, registered naturopath, The Australian Sheepskin Company and International Metal Traders. Hell of a mixture.'

'IMT are at the end.' Debbie pointed to the east corner of the building.

'Did you ask anyone if they left a forwarding address?'

She nodded. 'The receptionist didn't even have a new phone number. All she knew was that the lease had been cancelled some time last week.'

'Maybe this wasn't such a good idea,' Redman said. 'For all we know they don't use outside cleaners. Or we've missed them.'

'No, we haven't. Look.'

A white van had drawn up at the kerb in front of them. The driver went to the rear door and began unloading an industrial vacuum-cleaner.

'OK,' Redman said. 'Let me do the talking.' He got out, waiting for Debbie before he walked over to introduce himself.

The man saw them coming. He was unshaven and had coloured tattoos on the backs of both hands.

'Hi there,' Redman said. 'My name's Richmond, John Richmond. This is my wife, Nancy. We're up here on business from Sydney.'

'Hello.' Debbie smiled. She seemed distracted by the tattoos.

'We've been trying to get hold of someone from International Metal Traders since Friday,' Redman explained. 'But the girl on the desk told us they'd pulled out.'

'I don't know anything about that, mate.' The man started to wheel the vacuum-cleaner across the sidewalk.

Redman produced his bill-fold. 'I need some information,' he said.

The cleaner stopped.

'I'm in the scrap business,' Redman said. 'You know, copper wire, lead, that sort of thing. Six days ago IMT mailed me a cheque for fifteen grand. That's a lot of money to me and Nancy. And do you know what happened?'

'Bad cheque,' the cleaner said. 'Tell me about it. Happens all the time.'

'Not to me it doesn't.' Redman opened the bill-fold. 'I'm going to find these cowboys and put their balls in a vice. Nobody stuffs me around like that.'

'You wanna see their office?'

Redman gave him two fifty-dollar notes. 'I figure it's worth a look. What do you think?'

'Help yourself.' The man pocketed the money. 'But I'll tell you now, you're not going to find anything.'

At first sight, the cleaner's prediction appeared to be correct. Unlike the other rooms inside the building, the IMT office was bare. No calendar hung on the wall, there was no blotter on the desk, and although someone had doodled extensively on the cover of the phone book, Redman searched in vain for a number or a name amongst the scribble. The desk drawers were equally sterile, containing nothing but some paper-clips and a broken stapler.

Only in one of the filing cabinets was there evidence of the office ever having been occupied. Lying in the bottom drawer under an empty box-file were a number of airline brochures and a leaflet of shipping departures and arrivals. Debbie found them, calling Redman over to see if he thought they were of any use.

He sifted through them, already certain there was nothing of any value in the office. After letting himself be talked into coming here, and having taken the precaution of bringing the *nguzunguzu* with him, Redman was disappointed. Not that they should have expected anything else, he thought. IMT were hardly going to leave a trail of aluminium dust behind them for someone to follow.

'Steven,' Debbie whispered. 'Look at this.'

She showed him a Qantas brochure. In the timetable section at the back, some of the international flights had been underlined in pencil.

Redman turned to another page, finding more flights which had been underlined.

'We'll take them.' He gathered up the brochures. 'I don't know what for, but we might as well. Come on, let's get out of here.'

The cleaner accompanied them to the front door. 'What are those?' he asked.

'Airline brochures.' Redman showed him.

'If they've done a runner overseas you can kiss your money goodbye.' The cleaner ran his eyes over Debbie. 'You wanna be more careful.'

'Yes, I know. Thanks for your help, anyway.' She linked her arm into Redman's holding on to him while they walked back to the car.

'Well, John,' she said. 'I hope you heard what that nice man had to say.'

'It's tough in the scrap business.' He was reluctant to let go of her. 'Where shall we eat?'

'You choose.'

'There's a restaurant I know on the waterfront,' he said. 'I'll drive if you like.'

'Don't you think we should go back to Owen's place? So he can go through these brochures with us.'

'No,' Redman said.

'All right.' She pulled her arm away and gave him the car keys.

He drove automatically, thinking more about Debbie Hinton than the brochures she was holding in her lap. No matter how innocent his intentions, whenever he touched her it was the same. Everything was fine until she realized what was happening – until she somehow realized Redman himself was aware of the contact – that was the signal for her to draw away, almost as though he'd made a pass at her.

Perhaps it was an unconscious reaction, he thought. Perhaps she was so sick of men staring at her that she did it without knowing – treating him as she would treat Owen or anyone else who looked sideways at her.

The possibility of her regarding his motives as being no different to Owen's bothered Redman for much of the journey across town and it was still hovering in the back of his mind when they reached the restaurant.

But there, walking across the car-park, as if to confuse him, she took his arm again, this time continuing to hold it until they were inside.

Their table was on a balcony, overlooking a small garden. A string of outside lights, hanging from the trees, ran from the balcony rail to the water's edge.

'This is lovely.' She sat down.

'The food's good, too,' he said.

'The staff here won't recognize you, will they? Because of the article in the newspaper, I mean.'

Redman had forgotten the police were searching for him. He grinned at her. 'I'd better start being careful when I go out.'

'Do you want to see the brochures now? Before we order.'

'I suppose,' Redman said. 'What have we got?'

'Lufthansa, American Airlines, French UTA, Air New Zealand, Continental, Qantas and the leaflet on shipping.'

He picked one at random, a glossy American Airlines publication advertising Disneyland, the Grand Canyon and other attractions of the United States. Turning to the information section, he saw three of the flights had been underlined, two departures and one arrival. He examined the Continental brochure, finding four flights identified in the same manner.

Debbie had discovered a similar pattern in other brochures. She lay them open beside her on the tablecloth.

'Mostly flights from Sydney to Tokyo,' she said. 'Or the other way round.'

'There's one here from Darwin to Port Moresby in Papua New Guinea.' Redman turned the page. 'And another from Brisbane to Port Moresby that goes on to Manila.'

A waiter approached the table, a fresh-faced young man who smiled politely at Debbie while he looked for somewhere to put the menu.

'Oh, I'm sorry.' She began clearing the table.

'Hang on a second,' Redman said. 'Do you like seafood?'

'I like anything.'

Redman gave the waiter twenty dollars. 'Whatever you think is best,' he said. 'The wine as well. Is that OK?'

'Certainly, sir. Would you care for a drink before your meal?'

Redman glanced at Debbie. She wasn't listening, too busy with one of the brochures to have heard the question.

'We'll wait for the wine, thanks,' he said.

Debbie tore out a page and held it up in front of her. Then she took another brochure, turning quickly to the back of it.

'ABE,' she said. 'You're not going to believe this.'

Redman had no idea what she was talking about.

She passed him the page she'd torn out. It was a map of the South Pacific showing Qantas flight routes. They were marked in green, a series of long, curved lines joining cities on different continents.

'Hold it up to the light,' she said. 'Look off the east coast of Malaita in the Solomons, half-way down the island, about a quarter of an inch out to sea.'

He followed her instructions, seeing the pinhole in the paper at once.

'Now put the page down – so the light falls on it at an angle.' She leaned across. 'See?'

Surrounding the hole was the impression of a circle – a faint imprint left behind by pressure from a pencil or a ball-point pen. from the look of it, Redman guessed someone had used a compass to draw the circle on a sheet of tracing-paper that had been placed over the map beforehand.

'That's the first explosion,' Debbie said quietly. 'It's in range of the crop dusters, isn't it?'

He checked the scale on the map. 'About ninety miles offshore,' he said. 'A hundred and eighty mile round trip. AT 302s would manage that easily.'

'Did you see the letters and the date?' She used her fork as a pointer. 'The date's about right too.'

At the bottom of the circle, just inside it, were the equally faint imprints of the three capital letters ABE. Beneath them, in smaller print, someone had written March 7th – 14th.

Redman studied the letters trying to think what they might stand for, wondering why there was no pinhole nor a circle to mark the scene of the explosion which had destroyed Warren Decker's Eagle. Looking further off the Malaita coast for something which might identify the location of the second explosion, he was struck by the lack of flights in the region. It was then he realized why certain arrivals and departures in the brochures had been underlined.

He checked to see if he was right, interrupting Debbie when she began to speak.

'Got it,' he said. 'It's only those flights that go near the circle which are marked. The shipping routes are the same. IMT needed to know what ships and what aircraft would be in the area – and when they'd be there – so the explosion could be triggered at the best time to reduce the risk of anyone seeing it.'

'I know.' She smiled. 'Have you finished? Is it my turn now?'

'Sorry. What?' He was still thinking.

Delivery of their first course forced her to contain her excitement until the waiter had gone again. Then she dropped her bombshell.

'Darwin to Port Moresby,' she said. 'That flight doesn't go anywhere near the Solomon Islands. Nor do the flights between Brisbane and Manila.' She gave Redman the Continental brochure, already open at the right page.

This time he didn't bother to look for a pinhole. Instead he searched for another circle, expecting to find it hidden in the spider-web of flight patterns over the ocean.

He was wrong. Far from the Solomons, over a thousand miles away from Malaita, this circle was centred over land, on the west coast of Australia's Cape York peninsula. Inside the circle were the letters GBE. The writing was barely discernible, just clear enough for Redman to pick out the date below the letters.

He hadn't started on his appetizer. Now he forgot about it altogether.

'What's today?' he said.

'The 9th.' Debbie looked at him. 'Four days from now it's supposed to begin – whatever GBE is. Sometime between May 13th and May 20th.'

'You know what it is,' he said. 'We both know.'

'Another explosion. There's going to be another one.'

He nodded. 'A third one.'

'Do you know what ABE stands for?' she asked. 'Or GBE?'

'No. But I can guess why the dates span a seven-day period. It's a window of time – to allow for the right weather. IMT need a cloudy day without any wind.'

'You sound like Owen.' She started eating oysters, her eyes watching him as he carried on searching for anything that might reveal the location of the second Solomon Island explosion. There was nothing. No pinhole, no circle, no date. It was as if the second explosion had never taken place.

Redman tidied up the brochures, stacking them in a pile on an empty chair. He knew very well what she was waiting for him to say, but his head was buzzing and he was reluctant to commit himself.

Too much had happened in too short a time, he thought. What was supposed to have been a simple enquiry into the crash of the Airtech Eagle had turned out to be an investigation of impossible complexity. And in the middle of it all, had tripped Debbie Hinton. She, more than anything, was making it difficult for him to think clearly, particularly because she was expecting him to translate this evening's findings into a future which, if he decided to go ahead, was likely to be more uncertain than it was already.

He only partly enjoyed the meal, drinking too much wine while he tried to decide what he should do. By 11.30, with the restaurant empty, he was ready with his strategy. It lacked originality but Redman was in no mood to refine his ideas. Nor was he concerned about involving Debbie further in the puzzle. Like Owen she was already involved, already a part of it. But in what way she would continue to be a part of it, he was not yet sure.

Debbie herself seemed content to leave the question of what they should do next until after they left the restaurant, or even perhaps for another occasion. Over the last hour she had chatted about her job at WPA,

described her assignment in the Middle East, and twice
asked Redman questions he would rather not have
answered. He'd told her about Josie at the weekend, in
response to a direct enquiry, but as he had done then,
tonight he had skirted around the death of his wife,
bringing the conversation back to the present as quickly
as he could.

The waiter came to ask if they were ready for coffee.

'I know it's late,' Redman said, 'but could we have it in
the garden? Do you mind?'

'Not a problem.' The waiter checked to see if the
balcony door was unlocked. 'I'll bring it to you there.'

Debbie followed Redman outside onto the lawn. For
early autumn it was quite cool with a breeze ruffling the
leaves of a big gum tree.

Redman leaned against it, slightly heady from the wine.
This was the time, he thought. If the *nguzunguzu* was still
working, this would be the time.

'If we go up the peninsula, we go on my terms,' he said.
'All we do is look.'

'And take photographs.'

'For your story?'

'Not just that. If we have photographs, you can prove
what IMT are doing – what they were doing in the
Solomons. Do you think we'd be able to find the right
place?'

'I don't know. The whole peninsula is a wilderness. It's
not much different to the Solomons – forest, rivers,
mangroves and swamp. That's why IMT have chosen it.
They might as well have stayed in Malaita.'

'They couldn't,' she said. 'You interrupted them. They
killed Jennifer Decker but they didn't kill you. They've
had to find somewhere else.'

Redman shook his head. 'IMT have been planning this
for months – long before I got in the way. They bought the
crop dusters over a year ago and you said it's ten months
since they bought the squid boat in Hong Kong. Owen's

right. This is a huge operation.'

'So why have IMT closed down their office here?'

'Because they don't need it anymore. The planning's finished. Four days from now, or whenever the weather's all right, there's another experiment, then it's over.'

She smiled. 'What is?'

'I wish the hell I knew.' Redman looked at her directly. She was standing close to him, her face in shadow so he couldn't see her expression.

'Look,' he said, 'There's something I have to do, to get things straight before we go up north.'

'What?'

He reached out and untied the ribbon in her hair.

'Is that it?' she asked.

His hands still rested on her shoulders. He left them there, expecting her to remove them.

'Answer me,' she said.

'No,' Redman said. 'That's not it. That's not the half of it.'

Gently he pulled her towards him. He could feel her trembling and see how wide her eyes were open.

When he kissed her she froze, keeping her arms rigid by her side to show him his advance had been rejected.

Redman let her go. She was crying.

'Oh Christ, I'm sorry.' He was almost too embarrassed to apologize.

'You don't understand.' Seizing his hands she forced them back behind her neck. Then she kissed him, open-mouthed, using her whole body to crush him against the tree.

He could taste her tears, smell the fragrance of her hair. Both her arms were round him now, kissing him so fiercely that when she finally pulled away there was blood on his lip.

He was out of breath, bewildered as much by the delay in her response as he was by the intensity of it. Instead of misreading her, he'd been stupid – too absorbed with his own feelings to understand she'd been waiting for him to kiss her, waiting to show him that she wanted him as much as he wanted her.

Taking the ribbon from his hand, she used it to wipe his lip.

'Is there anything else you have to do?' she said softly.

He didn't answer. For a second her face had been blurred with an image of Josie, a superimposed image of a past he had thought would never go away. Now, for the first time in two years, he believed it might.

'There's nothing wrong, is there?' she asked.

'No.' He wound his fingers into her hair. 'No. There's nothing wrong at all.'

Five

The road was deteriorating. In place of the ruts and washboard of the last twenty miles was an undulating surface of hidden wash-outs and bottomless, sand-filled potholes. Twice in the past hour, Redman had nearly lost the Trooper in patches of sand that had given no warning of their softness, and twice he had only narrowly avoided trees after the truck had lurched unexpectedly to one side.

He was driving more cautiously now, at under ten miles an hour in four-wheel-drive, no longer prepared to trust his instincts. At the lower speed, although the ride was rougher, the Trooper was more controllable, handling the conditions easily in the lower gear.

Redman had given up wondering whether they would've been better off with a Range Rover. At this time of year, when the rivers were still running high along the peninsula, he knew there was no guarantee a vehicle of any kind would make it to where they were going. The hire company had even been reluctant to let them have the Trooper, pointing out that its use was restricted to journeys north no further than the Musgrave sheep station or the old gold-mining settlement at Coen.

They'd spent last night at Coen, sleeping in the back of

the truck after the 300 mile trip from Cairns – an exhausting drive, but one which had given Redman the opportunity to collect his thoughts. But this morning, setting off on unmarked roads to a destination that was no more definite than a pinhole on a map, he was less clear in his mind about Debbie and what they were doing than he had been yesterday.

It was still happening, Redman thought. No sooner had he got a fix on things, or believed he had, than something else came along to confuse him again. First it was Owen's new information about the dust, then it was Debbie last night when they had made love for the first time.

He glanced across at her. She was still asleep, insensitive to the bouncing and lurching, her head resting on a rolled-up sleeping-bag she'd wedged against the window. Already he wanted to touch her again, remembering the feel of her skin against his fingertips.

Distracted by the thought, he pulled over and parked the Trooper in the shade of some trees. When Debbie showed no signs of waking, he got out, leaving the door ajar so as not to disturb her.

To the south the peninsula was an unbroken panorama of forest, turning gradually from green to a hazy blue on the horizon. For a moment he was elsewhere, watching the coastline of Malaita slip away while the *Kwaibala* headed out to sea from Auki. The atmosphere was nearly the same, but the colours were different.

His mood was different too, he realized. Everything was different, which was why he was not sure what he was doing here. Owen had said they were crazy to attempt the trip, a statement he'd repeated several times before they left. Then, it had been easy to ignore the advice. Now, though, Redman believed there was another option.

He heard the click of the Trooper's door. It was followed by a shout.

Debbie walked over, shaking her arm. 'I got a shock off the door handle,' she said.

'Static electricity,' Redman grinned. 'It's good for you.'

'Are we lost?' she asked.

'Not yet. I needed a break – to do some thinking.'

'What about?'

'You and me; what Owen said about the dust in the seat squab being different to the dust at the airstrip; why we're in a tropical forest on a road that probably doesn't go anywhere.'

She sat down cross-legged on the sand to face him. 'Forget IMT, you mean.'

'Why not?'

She sighed. 'We've been through this before. Because IMT killed Jennifer Decker and tried to kill you. Because you have nothing to tell the police that they'll believe. Because someone has to find out what's happening. Because we decided.'

'They're not reasons. Not if you stand back and try to decide where we want to end up – you and I.'

Debbie picked up a handful of sand, letting it sift through her fingers. 'Do you know where you want to end up?'

'Depends how you feel.'

'I don't know how I feel. You're muddling me. One minute we're driving up the Cape York peninsula, the next minute we're talking about living happily ever after.' She reached out and took his hands in hers. 'I don't think this is a fairy-tale.'

'It's whatever we make it. We can either go on, or decide to do something else.'

'We can do both, can't we, finish what we've started? We'll be out at the coast before dark if the road doesn't get worse and as long as we don't have to cross more rivers.'

'Yeah, I guess.' He pulled her to her feet. 'As long as there aren't any more rivers to cross.'

For the next fifty miles the road remained passable, winding from one ridge to another through landscape that became progressively more spectacular and more desolate as they continued pressing westwards towards the Gulf.

By mid-afternoon they began to climb through a more rugged countryside, on a survey track which occasionally opened out into barren, treeless clearings before it again became almost indistinguishable from the surrounding terrain.

According to their map, the track was not recommended for vehicles travelling alone. The map also warned of swamps, estuarine crocodiles, poisonous stone fish, stinging jelly fish and other local hazards – not a region for the faint-hearted, Redman thought. Which is why no one ever came here, why there were no roads and why IMT had chosen it as the site for their third experiment.

Shortly before six o'clock the track petered out completely. Ahead lay a wilderness of savanna woodland, and somewhere in the distance, the Gulf of Carpentaria.

He had never been anywhere like this before. Because the latitude was nearly the same, he had expected the west coast of the peninsula to be similar to Malaita. Instead, he had the impression of being land-locked on a vast uninhabited continent in another world.

When he switched off the Trooper's engine, the silence was overwhelming.

'We're the only people who've ever been here,' Debbie said. 'I know we are.' She was smothered in sand and her face and her arms were streaked with dust. 'Where in God's name are we?'

Redman showed her on the map. 'I figure we're two or three miles from the coast. Round about here.'

Debbie saw his hands were blistered. She made him show her his palms.

'Steering-wheel,' Redman said. 'Kicks like a bastard when you hit a soft patch.'

'It's the grit. The whole truck's full of it.'

'So is your hair.'

'I know. I need a shower.' She studied the map. 'If

we're up high, between these two valleys, how are we going to get to the sea?'

'Walk. And hope the squid boat's anchored off the coast not too far away.'

'We could be miles from the right place,' she said. 'Miles and miles away. We might never find it.'

'Yeah.' He spat out a mouthful of sand, wondering if she realized how slim the chances really were. In country as tough as this, he thought, they'd be lucky to find the coast, let alone the squid boat.

Welcoming the opportunity to stretch his legs after two days behind the wheel, he went to explore, discovering at once why the track stopped here. They were indeed up high, on a small plateau flanked by inclines so steep that in several places the vegetation had failed to hold the hillsides together. A thousand feet below, at the foot of the slopes were graveyards of smashed and broken trees, protruding like tooth-picks from rubble on the valley floor.

Abandoning any idea of attempting to reach the coast from the northern or southern edges of the plateau, he walked west, searching for a more practical route.

He found it on the crest of a ridge at the plateau boundary, a pathway of bare rock no more than three or four feet wide. From where he stood, he fancied he could hear the sound of breakers.

He wandered back to find Debbie collecting twigs.

'No fire,' Redman said. 'If we're anywhere near where we think we are we don't want to make smoke signals.'

'No coffee then. And a cold dinner.' She glanced at him. 'Do you really believe we're close?'

'We'll know tomorrow. There's a trail of sorts, where the soil has been washed off the top of a ridge.'

'Let's go now. If I don't have to play cook, there's time before it's dark.'

'No.' He shook his head. 'You open some cans. I want to camouflage the truck – just in case.'

He worked steadily for the next two hours, building a canopy of branches, leaving Debbie to prepare their meal and find space inside the Trooper to spread out their sleeping-bags for the night.

They ate at dusk on a soft, warm evening, listening to the sound of insects in the bush, counting the stars as they came out one by one. Debbie gave up when she reached a hundred.

She sat now on the tail-gate, humming to herself while she watched Redman stack water containers and cans of spare fuel under a separate canopy of brushwood.

'Two weeks ago I wasn't even in Australia,' she said.

'Two weeks ago I'd never heard of Jennifer Decker.'

'Owen said he thought you liked her. Did you want to sleep with her?'

The question caught him wrong-footed. 'I only knew her for three days. What else did Owen say?'

She smiled. 'He told me to be careful of you.'

Redman pushed her back into the truck.

'No. Stop it, please.' She struggled to sit up again. 'It's not dark enough. I told you last night.'

'You didn't explain why.'

'I can't. Anyway, you haven't explained about Josie.' She hesitated. 'Tell me now.'

Redman took a deep breath. 'We'd been married four months. Hawthorne had just been promoted to vice-president at Airtech and Josie was teaching at a primary school in San Francisco. In February, half the kids in her class got sick with some kind of flu. Josie came home one Friday with it. She had a fever and a headache.'

'Go on.' Debbie drew a finger along his arm.

'That Saturday I was scheduled to fly out to Germany. Hawthorne thought he'd landed an order for twelve planes and Airtech needed someone over there in a hurry. I told them I couldn't go because Josie was ill, but she wouldn't hear of it. She said it was nothing and that she'd arranged for her mother to come over. Then Airtech put the pressure on. Hawthorne made it pretty clear that if I didn't go, I could look for another job.'

'So you went.'

'Yeah, I went. On Monday morning I got a call at my hotel in Dusseldorf to say Josie was in hospital. She died that night – while I was on a plane home.'

'That's awful.' Debbie kept her eyes lowered. 'What was it?'

'Meningitis. She'd tried to reach the phone in the hall but never made it. Her mother found her Sunday morning. But it was too late. It was my fault, you see.'

'It wasn't your fault. You didn't know.'

Fifty yards away, a dingo squealed. It made Redman jump.

Debbie waited nearly a minute before she made him look at her. 'It's dark now,' she murmured.

'You don't have to help me forget Josie. You've already done that.'

'I know.' She put a finger on his lips. 'Make me forget what I have to forget.'

This time when Redman pushed her back, she lay still, waiting for him to undress her. Last night she'd been reticent, giving the impression she was frightened, either of him or, in some peculiar way, of herself. But this evening there was no such reservation in her manner.

She was as eager as he was, freed by the darkness from whatever had made her hold back earlier. Soon she began to tremble, whispering his name and telling him she could not wait.

Intoxicated by her, unable to think of anything but the blinding pleasure of taking her completely, Redman began to drown. He was lost, equally unwilling to wait, driven on by her cries as she reached her climax before he was overtaken by his own shuddering release of passion.

Afterwards, for over an hour, they lay together listening to the night sounds from the bush, each reluctant to break the spell between them. Only when mosquitoes started to invade the truck did Redman get up to close the doors.

Outside to the west, a bank of cloud had started to drift across the stars. A cloudy day tomorrow might do it, he thought. But until then he was certain the spell would hold.

Shaken awake at dawn, Redman's first concern was not the weather but the expression of alarm on Debbie's face. She was sitting up in her sleeping-bag, holding one of the Trooper's doors open with her foot. Echoing from the northern valley was the unmistakable chop of a helicopter rotor.

'Shit.' He tried to estimate how far away it was. 'When did you hear it?'

'A minute ago. It woke me up.'

He jumped out of the truck, intending to clear up evidence of their evening meal and add more branches to the canopy while there was still time. Before he could do either, the rotor noise became much louder.

Flying parallel to the ridge on which the plateau stood, the helicopter was gaining altitude. At any second Redman expected it to soar out of the valley in front of him.

A pair of lorikeets flashed by, disturbed by the noise. They were followed by budgerigars and several larger birds, all of them keeping low, skimming past the canopy as though it was invisible.

He retreated into the Trooper.

'How close is it?' Debbie was still struggling into her clothes.

'I can't see. It's down in the valley somewhere. We might be all right, though. The canopy's pretty good on that side. None of the birds are taking any notice of it.'

'Birds don't carry machine-guns.' She shivered. 'We know we're in the right place now, don't we?'

The noise was fading. Redman could hear the beating of the rotor moving further up the valley.

When he got out of the truck for the second time, he remembered to look at the sky. Except for some wisps across the morning sun, it was cloudless – a sign of a free day, he thought, provided the helicopter kept away and as long as there weren't any crop dusters about.

It was mid-morning before Redman decided the helicopter was not going to return. There had been no sign of any other aircraft in the area, the wildlife on the plateau had settled down and he was as anxious as Debbie to make a move.

They left at ten, quickly discovering that the trail was not a trail at all. Redman's description of it had been right. It was no more than the crest of ridge, a meandering catwalk of varying width with the northern and southern valleys opening out on each side of it like the arms of a fan.

The further they walked the more sparse became the savanna woodland, now and again affording them views of distant slopes and of river flats indented by estuaries and streams. Occasionally they came across flowering tropical trees and twice saw wedgetail eagles spiralling upwards on air currents until they were lost to sight. Debbie had given up trying to photograph them, concentrating instead on birdwing butterflies and on keeping her footing as the trail became steeper.

For nearly half a mile the trail wound downwards, taking them closer to the sound of surf but denying them any glimpse of the sea itself. Soon the ridge flattened out, curving on to a promontory of grassy mounds and sand-filled hollows. And there, at last, for as far as they could see, the deep azure blue of the Gulf of Carpentaria stretched away before them.

To their right was the mouth of the northern valley, cut in half by the river flats and bounded by a beach of pure white sand – a sprawling tapestry of the Queensland Gulf coast, marred by the presence of what appeared to be a full-scale military operation.

Two ships were anchored off the coast, a heavy truck was grinding up the river-bed and, in shallow water at the river-mouth, men were unloading a tractor from a landing-craft. Nearby, like toys left behind by children on the beach, a helicopter stood beside two AT 302 crop dusters.

'GBE,' Redman said quietly. 'We're on top of it.'

'Not quite.' Debbie's face was flushed. 'We're not close enough.' She handed him her camera. 'You look first.'

Through the telephoto lens he could pick out more detail and gain a better idea of distance. The river-mouth was around two and a half miles away, he decided, with the valley extending inland four or five times that far – far enough to explain why the circles in the brochures were not centred on the coast itself.

'Well?' Debbie was waiting for him to say something.

Before he returned the camera, he swung the lens on to the larger of the two ships. The stern gaped open, like the mother-ship of a whaling fleet. A transporter, Redman thought, IMT's transporter for the landing-craft, the truck, the aircraft and the rest of the equipment.

He imagined the smaller ship was the *Zhongshan*, a rusty, nondescript vessel moored nearer to the beach. It was surrounded by an oil slick in which dozens of drums were floating – the same kind of drums he'd found in a derelict hut in another country a thousand miles away.

'We can't stay here,' Redman said. 'It's too exposed.' He gave Debbie the camera.

'We can't see anything from anywhere else. Shall we try and get down to the beach?'

He went to reconnoitre, discovering that the prom-ontory was nothing more than a gigantic sand-dune. Below him, apart from outcrops of rock and lumps of sandstone, the beach was bare of cover. It would also make a poor vantage point compared with the promontory.

He walked back to Debbie. She was lying on one of the mounds busy with her camera.

'No good,' Redman said. 'We'll have to dig in here.'

'Here?'

He kicked at the sand in one of the hollows. 'We've got spades in the truck. I just hope we're not being stupid. Owen said we should keep ten miles away.'

She rolled to one side leaving the camera on the mound. 'Have a look. Tell me how far that is.'

Framed in the view-finder was a picture of the river-flats at the head of the valley. Through the shimmer of heat-haze Redman could see the truck parked at the base of a tall steel pylon.

'Seven or eight miles,' he said.

'Not nine or ten?'

'I don't know. It's a fair way, though. I suppose it depends on what type of dust IMT are going to use – whether it's been treated with that chemical Owen found in the seat-squab dust.'

She frowned. 'I can't see what difference a chemical makes. I don't even know what it is.'

'It's an oxidizing agent – magnesium perchlorate – to add oxygen to the fireball. You can do two things with an explosive dust, either make it safer by adding something that doesn't burn, like powdered rock, which is what they do in coal mines, or you can make it more dangerous.'

'And adding an oxidizing agent makes it more dangerous?'

'A hell of a lot more. Owen said he wouldn't light a cigarette anywhere near dust that was laced with magnesium perchlorate.'

'Well, I'll go down to the beach and ask what they're using, shall I?'

He grinned. 'Ask about the pylon, too. We need to know if that's going to be the centre of the blast.'

'Do you think it is?'

'Yes, I do.' He stood up and pulled her to her feet. 'We'd better move in case that helicopter takes off again. We'll come back tomorrow and dig ourselves a foxhole. Nothing's going to happen today. The sky's too clear.'

'All right.' She began brushing the sand off her clothes, wriggling away laughing when he started to help by picking grass out of her blouse.

'If you ask me nicely, I'll rig up a shower from one of the water containers,' he said. 'We can use it after dark.'

She looked at him suspiciously. 'Why do I have this feeling I won't be any safer back at camp than I am here?'

'It'll be a cold shower,' Redman said. 'Trust me.'

The fourth day dawned cloudy. It was also windless. On the promontory, instead of the air being thick with wind-blown sand as it had been yesterday, this morning the atmosphere was hot and still. The surf too was still, breaking in a line of foam three or four hundred yards out from the river-mouth on a sand-bar exposed by the low tide.

To the north, for the first time since they'd been here, there were no shadows in the valley, and no sunlight reflecting off the river.

The dull conditions had made it safe to erect the periscope – a crude assembly of sticks into which Redman had lashed the driving mirrors from the truck. Although it worked well enough, until this morning he had avoided using it because of the risk of sunshine glinting off the glass.

Lying on his back in the foxhole, he adjusted the lower mirror so he could see the beach.

'Signs of life?' Debbie enquired.

'They're refuelling the helicopter. Have a look.' He checked his watch, wondering if today was going to be different.

Each morning at eight o'clock for the last three days the helicopter had taken off to conduct what seemed to be a routine search of the valley before commencing its shuttle service between the mother-ship and the pylon. But the last three days had been cloudless, Redman thought. Today had to be different.

Debbie withdrew the periscope, pulling the cover of woven branches back over the foxhole. 'The helicopter's coming,' she said. 'And the squid boat's moving.'

It was the news Redman had been waiting for. Unfolding the chart Owen had prepared, he checked the estimated arrival times for today's flights.

'You don't have to do that again,' Debbie said. 'We already know when its safest.'

'Safe for IMT or safe for us?'

'You know what I mean.' She took the chart from him. 'The best time is after midnight.'

'We know it won't be in the dark because of the flash. Owen's sure. He said some satellites can even detect flashes in daylight whether there's cloud or not.'

'It'll be between nine-thirty and midday, then. After the Darwin flight and before the one from Guam.'

The helicopter was approaching. Redman had a glimpse of it through the branches. It was a Hughes 500, the civilian equivalent of the military Cayuse, heading straight up the valley instead of carrying out the search pattern he'd expected.

As soon as it had gone he climbed from the foxhole and looked out to sea. Followed by the *Zhongshan*, the mother-ship was underway now, sailing south in a haze of dirty smoke – another sign that today was the day.

He turned his attention inland, where, at the head of the valley, the helicopter was already hovering above the pylon. Doing what? he wondered. What was the purpose of the pylon?

Debbie clambered out of the hole and began setting up her camera on one of their water containers. He watched her, wishing he'd met her in some other way. Despite the hours she'd spent below ground, her face and arms were browner, and the sun had begun to bleach her hair. She reminded Redman of another time, of long forgotten summers misspent with fair-haired girls a million years ago when life had been much simpler.

'Are you going to leave the camera there?' he asked.

She nodded. 'It's got an automatic shutter. All we have to do is switch it on.'

Taking one of the spades, he shovelled sand around the container, building a mound at the rear of it before hammering in a palisade of sticks for reinforcement.

'The blast won't be that bad,' she said. 'Not here. We're miles away.'

'Why do you think the ships are pulling out?'

'You're trying to frighten me.'

'No I'm not. The valley's a funnel. If we're right, if they're going to trigger the explosion by a dynamite charge on the pylon, the shock wave can only go in two directions – either straight up or straight out to sea.'

'What about us then?'

'We keep our heads down.' Redman's voice lacked confidence.

'Look.' She pointed.

The helicopter was returning, skimming at low altitude over the river-flats until it reached the beach. It circled twice then carried on out to sea, heading towards the mother-ship.

Redman was still watching it when he heard a less familiar noise.

Debbie knelt down to look through the lens of the camera. 'It's the truck,' she said. 'But it's not going anywhere.'

For the entire time they'd been here, just as the crop dusters had remained on the beach, the truck had remained parked beneath the pylon. Until today Redman had given it little thought. Now he began to understand.

He knelt down beside her. 'Let me see,' he said.

Smoke was rising from the pylon, billowing from the top of it.

The throb of the truck engine became a roar, the sound of a big diesel under load. And mixed with it was another sound. Redman recognized it immediately.

Closing off his mind to what he guessed was happening on the beach, he peered through the view-finder, concentrating on the pylon.

Spreading out rapidly across the head of the valley, the smoke was obscuring everything. He could just distinguish the pylon and the outline of the truck, but the hills beyond were gone, masked by wreathing, dull grey clouds.

It wasn't smoke. Redman knew exactly what it was. The smoke was dust – spewing from the top of the pylon at the rate of hundreds of cubic feet per second. IMT had outgrown the open spaces of the Pacific. For this, the third test, their plans were more ambitious.

Debbie grabbed his shoulder. 'The dusters,' she said.

'I know.' He was trying to think, trying to decide whether there was time for them to reach the Trooper and whether it would make any difference if they did.

Both AT 302s were taxiing along the hard sand near the water. Redman saw the first one stop by the tractor to receive its cargo of dust from the loading bucket.

Debbie was alarmed by the expression on his face. 'What is it?' she said.

'They're filling the valley. The truck engine is driving a pump or a fan. That's dust coming out of the pylon – tons and tons of it.'

'They can't,' she said. 'It isn't possible.'

'Yes it is. This is the big one. They're going to trigger an air blast to ignite a whole valley full of dust.' He paused. 'The coal-mine effect – the valley's one huge coal mine.'

On the beach there was a rasping whine from the propeller of the first duster as the pilot began his take-off. A moment later the AT 302 was airborne. It flew out to sea, followed by its companion, gaining altitude before both planes turned to make their first run up the valley.

'Get in the foxhole,' Redman instructed.

Debbie was frightened. She crouched inside while Redman pulled the roof of branches into place.

He gave her one of the spades. 'Dig,' he said. 'Dig like hell.'

Her eyes met his. 'How deep do we have to be?'

He didn't answer. By sliding the periscope upwards and wedging it against a tree root he had a general view of the valley. The AT 302s were busy discharging dust, flying alongside each other at what he thought was about 1500 feet. They peeled off at the head of the valley, returning to land on the beach where their pay-loads were replenished from the stack of drums around the tractor.

In between helping Debbie he watched them for nearly an hour, counting the number of trips they made so he could mentally add each load to the quantity of dust he thought was coming from the pylon.

When eventually he swung the periscope inland, the pylon itself had vanished.

Redman felt his stomach knot.

From one side of the valley to the other the air had turned grey. A wall of cloud was drifting upwards, spilling over the ridges like milk boiling from a saucepan. And above the wall hung the airborne layers spread by the dusters. He could see each one, motionless layers suspended in the air thousands of feet above the valley floor, waiting for the signal which would bring them to life.

The AT 302s were coming back. On each occasion they were higher, always flying side by side to release their dust into the atmosphere.

He gave up trying to calculate how much dust had already been dispersed. It was too much – more than Owen's wildest estimate – enough, Redman knew, to create a fireball of unimaginable proportions.

Although Debbie was still working, she was making little headway with the excavations. Hard, compacted sand had given way to stone and gravel in the bottom of the foxhole. She was filthy and streaked in perspiration.

Redman took over. In order to avoid thinking about

what was going to happen, he dug furiously, using the spade as an axe until the handle broke. The shaft on the other spade proved equally fragile, snapping off at the blade when he attempted to lever out a block of solid sandstone.

Oblivious of his bleeding hands, he leaned against the wall of the hole, trying to think what else he could do.

'How many more times have the planes come over?' he asked.

'Four, I think.' Debbie was biting her lip. 'I've been going by the noise. I can't see them anymore.'

'Well they can't see us either, then.' He pushed the branches away and climbed out.

Below him, waves were still breaking on the sand-bar, the only disturbance on a flat, featureless sea that extended westwards to meet the sky at an overcast horizon. Of the two ships, there was no sign.

To the north where the valley had once been, there was nothing. An enormous curtain had been drawn across the valley mouth. Over 3,000 feet high and nearly five miles wide, the curtain was fluid, beginning to roll on to the beach and continuing to flow across the trail leading to the promontory.

Redman could smell it, a dirty metallic smell which was already making him feel queasy. Because the dust was laced, he wondered? Or because he was frightened half to bloody death.

Debbie clambered out to join him. She coughed when she tried to speak.

'Here.' He gave her his handkerchief to put over her nose and mouth.

'My God.' She was overawed by what she saw. 'We're too close,' she breathed. 'We're much too close.'

He nodded.

'How long?'

'Soon.' He pointed.

One of the planes had landed on the beach, this time

not for more dust but to collect the tractor driver and another man. The second AT 302 was departing, flying out to sea, tipping its wings as it passed over the sand-bar.

The noise of its propeller had barely died away when the truck engine stopped, leaving the valley in silence.

'This is it.' Redman switched the camera on to automatic.

'Tell me we'll be all right,' Debbie said.

'We'll be all right.' He smiled at her. 'Better get ready.'

Inside the foxhole he made her lie down in the rubble, then scraped handfuls of sand over her until she was covered completely except for her face.

She tried to turn her head towards him. 'Aren't you scared?' she whispered.

'Yes.' Redman covered her eyes with his hands. 'Oh yes. I'm scared.'

Six

Four and a half miles out to sea, the Hughes was stationary at an altitude of 9,000 feet when the pilot received the first enquiry over his radio. He checked his instruments before replying, but forgot to mention the cameras.

The second communication from the mother-ship was terse, instructing him to repeat his position and provide immediate confirmation of the video channel status.

He reported that the pictures on both screens were clear then attempted to overcome his nervousness. Today, because he was closer to the site and because his responsibilities were greater than they had been for the two air-burst tests, he was apprehensive – so much so, that over the last hour one of his hands had begun to shake.

Ahead of him the peninsula was featureless, a drab stretch of coastline set against an uncharacteristically washed-out sky. He could pick out the whiteness of the beach and what he thought was a line of waves breaking on the sand-bar, but the mouth of the target valley itself was indistinct.

His radio crackled again. Starting to reply in Arabic, he

reverted quickly to English, stating he was prepared to start the countdown as soon as the arming signal was transmitted.

It came quickly enough, a pale green bulb flashing at one second intervals on his instrument panel.

At initiation minus ten, the pilot became busier. He checked the video channels again, switched on the recorders for the blast sensors and pulled the visor down over his helmet. Finally he adjusted his harness, pulling the webbing tight across his chest.

His finger was ready now, waiting for the light to change from green to red. At initiation minus two he stopped breathing. Then he pressed down on the button.

On the seaboard of Cape York a beacon flashed, a pin-prick of light high above the peninsula. From it came horizontal streaks of lightning. They were a vivid red, illuminating the valley in an unearthly crimson glow until two of the airborne layers ignited simultaneously. For an instant the sky turned white, irradiating the sea, the beach and thirty miles of coastline. Then, in a flash of blazing incandescence, the remainder of the dust exploded.

An inverted pyramid of fire burst from the valley-mouth. It was followed by waves of flame.

Over the peninsula the waves shot skywards while over the Gulf, channelled outwards by the valley walls, boiled a phosphorescent sphere of heat. It died, only to be re-ignited, driven on towards the helicopter by the expanding blast-front.

No longer mesmerized by the spectacle, the pilot panicked. Shouting over his radio, he put the Hughes into a climb, endeavouring to evade the approaching fireball.

The manoeuvre was unnecessary. For the briefest of moments the helicopter became unstable, swerving sideways like a dragonfly caught in a wind-gust before continuing to climb unharmed towards the clouds.

At the same time, rolling out across the Gulf of Carpentaria came a roar from the valley. It was muted, a deep, reverberating surge of noise created by an explosion not of great destructive force but of great size. The roar persisted for several seconds, abating only slowly until the peninsula and the Gulf were once again at peace.

The third Consortium experiment was over. Damage reconnaissance flights would reveal what proportion of the dust had ignited, but it was already clear how successful the test had been. Far from the political arena which had spawned the testing programme, a low-technology experiment had finally provided the answer to a high-technology problem, giving leaders in countries half a world away the means at last to challenge the power base of their stronger neighbour.

On board the mother-ship and on the deck of the squid boat, crew members removed their protective glasses before going below to inspect the telemetry data and view the video recordings.

For all but a handful of these men the explosion was of little consequence. Despite what they had just witnessed, their thoughts were centred more on the prospect of returning home to be reunited with their families than on the politics of international power, and soon, in the rush to complete Stage 2, the memories of a valley on the empty Queensland coast would be forgotten.

Important work remained to be done and, over the coming weeks and months, instead of today's test, it would be the results of a quite different explosion that the men of Project Omega would remember.

For two other people struggling to keep alive in a collapsed foxhole on the peninsula, today's test was far from over.

Choking with every breath, Redman was using the broken spade to clear an air-space around Debbie's face. She, too, was choking, spitting out mouthfuls of sand only to gag on the smoke which hung over the promontory like a blanket.

He used his hands, scrabbling away at the rubble until

he had freed one of her arms.

'Grab hold,' he shouted. 'Push with your other arm.'

Holding her wrist, Redman heaved upwards, partially dragging her from the sand.

'I can't hear you,' she said. 'My ears are ringing.'

'So are mine. Push for Christ's sake. The smoke's getting worse.' He used the spade again, this time to clear around his own legs.

The foxhole had nearly become their grave. Much of the north side had slumped inwards on top of them, burying Redman to the waist and covering Debbie completely. Yet, in spite of the collapse and their exposed position on the ridge, somehow they had survived the blast, the flying rocks and the searing wall of heat that had passed overhead at the moment of ignition.

Redman's recollection of the explosion was unclear. He'd seen the initial flash in the periscope but, after the first red bolts of lightning hit the ridge, he could remember little apart from thinking they would surely perish as the explosion proper took hold in the valley.

Now he was beginning to believe they had escaped only to be suffocated by smoke and unburned particles of dust.

He worked harder, using all his strength to haul Debbie free. Her face was white and her breathing was uneven.

'Truck,' Redman yelled. 'The valley's on fire.'

She nodded her head.

Once outside the foxhole, Redman was stunned by the extent of the devastation. The valley was black. So was the river, the beach and the sand-bar. Here and there, where the concentration of dust had been below the explosive limit, individual trees remained erect, leafless sentinels standing in an alien landscape of burning timber and smouldering heaps of brushwood.

As far as he could make out, most of the smoke appeared to have been generated by the combustion or partial combustion of the dust. The forest was not burning fiercely, although Redman could see areas of flame at the head of the valley where the temperature had been more severe. He wondered what chances there were of the Trooper being in one piece.

Still spitting, Debbie climbed from the hole and started looking for her camera. She found what was left of it buried in the mound of sand. Forcing open the back she removed the film before turning to inspect the valley.

'Come on.' Redman took the film away from her. 'We have to get out of here right now.'

She was speechless, staring first into the valley then up at a ragged gap in the clouds. The sunlight was pink, reflecting off the smoke, sparkling and dancing around the edges of the gap as though streams of coloured water were pouring upwards into the sky above.

He took her arm, forcing her to hurry. She stumbled along, coughing more as the trail became steeper, refusing Redman's help when she fell because he himself was coughing so badly that on two occasions she had to wait for him to catch his breath.

Further along the ridge, heat rising from the valley was creating an up-draught. It was carrying the smoke and dust away from the trail, leaving pockets of air that were sufficiently clean to breathe. They stopped in each pocket, gulping to clear their lungs before resuming their climb towards the plateau.

In front of them a dingo limped across the trail dragging a broken leg. Other animals appeared, heading for the safety of the southern valley; a kangaroo with a blackened coat, a snake which stopped transiently to look around before it slithered away into the undergrowth, and large numbers of birds that, by some means or other, had escaped the blast-wave and the flames.

On the plateau most of the trees were standing. At first sight the Trooper also appeared to be intact beneath its canopy of branches. Only on closer inspection was the extent of the damage obvious. Every window was shattered, the rear doors had been partially twisted off their hinges and a giant can opener had been at work on one side of the roof.

Redman turned the ignition key. He was rewarded by the heartening sound of the engine idling.

After pushing out what remained of the laminated windshield, he slid behind the wheel and kicked open the passenger door for Debbie.

She climbed in beside him holding a handkerchief over her nose.

'Can you hear any better?' Redman asked.

'A bit. The ringing's stopped.'

'OK – buckle up. There might be parts of the ridge on fire. I'm going to drive like hell.'

He engaged four-wheel-drive and dropped the clutch. The Trooper pushed out of the canopy leaving furrows from its wheels in the blackened sand as Redman put his foot down.

The track was free of blockages. For the first one or two miles they encountered splintered tree trunks and piles of branches, but for the most part, the survey track was either unobstructed or littered with debris that was too small to impede their progress.

Once his confidence returned Redman drove faster, sliding on the curves using every inch of the track to maintain speed until he was sure they were out of danger. Each mile away from the coast the air grew sweeter, and soon even the dirty metallic taste was gone.

Gradually he eased back on the throttle, relaxing for the first time since the explosion had hammered him face down into the foxhole. It was easier now for him to appreciate how miraculous their escape had been. Sheer good fortune, he wondered, the *nguzunguzu* or a low dust concentration on the promontory?

He forced himself to think of something else, trying to decide how best to dispose of the battered Trooper before they reached civilization and, how he was going to tell

Debbie what he planned to do.

For a while he thought of nothing at all, almost failing to recognize the end of the survey track when it opened out on to the much better surface of the road.

He looked across at Debbie intending to tell her the good news. She was sitting tight-lipped, gripping her seat-belt with both hands.

'Hey.' He squeezed her leg. 'We made it.'

'Owen was wrong,' she said.

'About us needing to be ten miles away?'

'No. About it being impossible to use dust as a bomb. I've never seen anything as terrible as that. I don't ever want to see anything like it again.'

'Here.' Redman passed her a water container. 'Wash some of the dust away. Empty it over your head.'

'Have we got enough to spare?'

He had no opportunity to reply.

Less than a hundred yards away at treetop level, an AT 302 screamed across the road.

'Oh my God.' Debbie shrank down in her seat. 'They've followed us.'

The furrows, Redman thought grimly. White furrows in blackened sand. He changed into third gear, trying to hold the Trooper in a straight line while he built up speed again.

'They can't stop us, can they?' Debbie said. 'The plane can't land on the road.'

Redman endeavoured to remember how large the clearings were. Could an experienced pilot put a duster down somewhere? Was the surface hard enough? Was the pilot armed?

The AT 302 was returning, heading directly for them in a dive. It flattened out, skimming twenty feet above the truck before entering a long curving climb. Redman heard the whine from the propeller as it passed overhead.

The Trooper was already on the limit, lurching from side to side at thirty miles an hour on a potholed road that was going to kill them if Redman wasn't careful.

Ahead lay one of the clearings. It was barely a hundred yards long, too short for the AT 302 to attempt a landing, Redman decided.

Shouting at Debbie to hang on, he increased speed to guard against the possibility of rifle shots from the air.

The truck was less than half-way to safety when Redman heard the whine again. This time the plane came from behind, flying slowly at low altitude while it discharged half a ton of explosive dust into the clearing.

An image of a different aircraft flashed into Redman's mind, of an Airtech Eagle detonating high above the ocean. Frantically he reached for the ignition key.

The Trooper lost all headway, slumping to a halt.

Debbie had one hand on the floor while she fought to unfasten her seat-belt with the other.

'Don't get out,' Redman yelled. 'Sparks. Static electricity.'

She continued fighting until Redman got a hand on the back of her jeans.

'Wait,' he shouted. 'Listen to me.'

He couldn't hold her. Coughing and retching she opened the door and put her feet on to the ground.

Nothing happened. Instead of an explosion a gale swept across the clearing, an enormous blast of air, diluting the dust and carrying it away.

Still holding Debbie's waistband Redman crawled across the seat. He got out of the truck on the passengers' side, not yet daring to release her.

Wide-eyed, she buried herself in his arms.

Above them, for a minute or two the Hughes continued to hover, using the down-draught from its rotor to scour the last vestiges of dust from the clearing before it landed fifty feet away in an innocent cloud of wind-blown sand.

Redman watched the rotor begin to slow. He felt sick and more frightened then he had been at the airstrip. As surely as IMT had found him on Malaita they had tracked him down again today. But today there was nowhere to go, no river, no rocks and no jungle.

The AT 302 was departing. In a repeat of his manoeuvre at the test-site the pilot tipped his wings in a signal of farewell before turning to commence his return journey to the beach.

Three men emerged from the helicopter. Two of them wore army fatigues contrasting with the white trousers and smart white shirt of their companion – a much taller, thinner man. They walked over to the Trooper.

Redman made Debbie stand behind him. He'd already seen that one of the men carried a machine-pistol.

'Is it him?' Debbie whispered. 'The tall man from the launch?'

'Don't do anything or say anything.' Redman gripped her hand.

'Well, well.' The tall man smiled pleasantly. 'I must say you look rather more the worse for wear than when I met you last, Mr Redman. On the other hand, after your recent experience I imagine you feel fortunate to be no more than travel-worn and dirty.' He looked at Debbie over Redman's shoulder. 'And who do we have here?'

Neither Debbie nor Redman answered.

'Allow me to express my surprise at your survival. My pilots tell me there is evidence of a shallow hole on a ridge overlooking the valley. Did you really shelter there?'

'Who are you?' Redman said. 'Who the hell are you?'

'Forgive me. I am Nassim Khatib. The gentleman with the gun is Mohammed Fawaz and my other colleague is Faisal Subhi.' The tall man was clearly interested in Debbie. 'Now please give me your name.'

'Debbie Hinton.' She moved to stand beside Redman. 'I'm a journalist.'

'I see. And what is a journalist like you doing on the Cape York peninsula?'

'For Christ's sake,' Redman said. 'You know damn well why we're here.'

'Indeed. But the intriguing question of who you are

working for remains unanswered. I have wondered a great deal about you, Mr Redman. Are you what you seem to be? Do you have some knowledge of the Omega Project? Is your name perhaps Friedman instead of Redman? Who has sent you here?'

The significance of the remarks was lost on Redman. He tightened his grip on Debbie's hand, struggling to steady his nerves.

'Are you by any chance Jewish, Mr Redman?'

'I'm part Cherokee Indian. What's it to you?'

Khatib appeared to lose patience. 'We are wasting time,' he said. 'See if the man is circumcised. It may tell us something.'

'Get lost,' Redman said. He started to kick out but was driven to his knees by a blow to the side of his head from a pistol butt.

The man called Fawaz dragged him over to the Trooper, sat him up against a rear wheel and proceeded to lash his hands behind him with a length of cord.

Only half conscious, Redman felt a hand groping between his legs. When he tried to resist he discovered his wrists had been tied to the wheel itself.

Fawaz completed his examination. 'He is not circumcised,' he called. 'I check the girl, yes?'

Khatib was unamused. Leaving Subhi to guard Debbie he came over to speak to Redman. 'Please listen carefully,' he said. 'I can either transport you and Miss Hinton to my ship for interrogation or we can both make this as quick and painless as I'm sure you wish it to be. I have a number of questions to which I require answers. Any refusal to co-operate will result in persuasion being applied not to you but Miss Hinton. Do you understand?'

Redman nodded.

'I am certain Miss Hinton would prefer us to complete our business here. In case you have overlooked the possibility, may I point out that the presence of an attractive girl on board my ship is likely to be upsetting both for you and for her. There is no need for me to paint a more graphic picture, is there?'

'No.' Redman tried unsuccessfully to think through a haze of pain.

'Apart from Airtech in California, who else do you work for?'

'No one.'

'What knowledge do you have of the Consortium – of the COAS?'

'I don't know what you mean.' Redman coughed up a lung-full of dust. Although his head was pounding and he couldn't see properly out of one eye, he sensed the questions were designed to lead him into a corner. They were too simple, and Khatib was too willing to accept the answers, Redman thought. Only by providing answers that created more questions could he stay alive and only by staying alive could he protect Debbie.

'Am I expected to believe that after travelling to the Solomon Islands in order to investigate the loss of Decker's aircraft you did no more than chance upon evidence of our airburst experiment there?'

Redman nodded. Whether Khatib used the word experiment instead of saying experiments, he wasn't sure. He wasn't sure of anything.

'Do you or Miss Hinton know what enhanced dust is? Are you familiar with the material known as magnesium perchlorate?'

'No.' The answer came easily, a response to some unconscious warning.

'By what means did you learn of our second experiment?'

It was a trap, Redman thought wildly. The second experiment in the Solomons or the third one here today? 'We raided the IMT office in Brisbane,' he said. 'There were brochures there – with pinholes in them.'

'I see'. Khatib raised his eyebrows. 'Well I never. How enterprising of you. But why risk your life and the life of the girl by coming here? What did you expect to accomplish?'

'Photos,' Redman said.

'Ah, of course. Where is the camera?'

'It got smashed.'

'But you have retained the film.'

Redman decided there was no advantage in lying. 'It's in the glove-compartment,' he said. 'Rolled up inside a map.'

Reaching through the Trooper's shattered window, Khatib withdrew the map.

'Let the girl go,' Redman said slowly. 'She's only along for the ride – to get the story for the papers. She can't hurt you. Neither of us can. We can't stop you doing whatever the hell it is you are doing.'

Khatib smiled. 'But if you are telling me the truth, you have no idea what it is you wish to stop. I am afraid I doubt your appreciation of our undertaking is as slight as you would like me to believe it is. Only an extremely foolish person would choose to meddle in something that is far beyond their comprehension. And I regret that you, Mr Redman, do not strike me as being foolish.'

Redman felt his stomach knot again. From the moment the dust had enveloped the truck he'd known their chances were all but gone. The execution at the airstrip was a forerunner of what was about to take place here. It didn't matter that he and Debbie were as ignorant of IMT's intentions as they had ever been. Nor did it matter whether Khatib believed they had some understanding of the background to the tests. Nothing was going to make any difference now.

'Bring the girl,' Khatib said. 'Tie her to the other wheel. Quickly.'

Debbie's face was a mask, an expression Redman had seen before, the frozen look he remembered from the evening at the restaurant. But today, the reason for it was different. Instead of apprehension it was hate, raw, undisguised hate. He could feel it, see it emanating from her eyes.

She twisted a hand in her pony-tail, staring coldly at Subhi while he escorted her to the truck.

'Sit,' Subhi instructed. 'You make it easy for me to tie you.'

She leaned against the wheel offering no resistance.

Redman could think of nothing to say which might reassure her. Yet she was no longer frightened, he realized. It was the dust that terrified her, the dreadful, suffocating wait for the instant of ignition. Now the dust was gone she was in control of herself again.

'And who is it you work for, Miss Hinton?' Khatib enquired.

'World Press Association.' She spoke quietly. 'If you kill us like you killed Jennifer Decker a hundred newspapers will print the story.'

'What story is that? Surely the loss of a light aircraft in the Solomon Islands is yesterday's news. And I am told the *Queensland Tribune* has concluded Mr Redman is responsible for Mrs Decker's death. Furthermore, I cannot believe any newspaper would be sufficiently motivated to investigate the disappearance of two people who have chosen to venture into the most desolate part of the Cape York peninsula by themselves.'

Redman had listened with a growing sense of helplessness. There was no conceivable reason why Khatib should release them. If the questions were finished, why was he delaying? Why not get it over with?

'It is necessary for me to radio my ship,' Khatib announced. 'You may talk to each other if you wish to do so.' He walked away.

Of the two men who remained behind, Fawaz was the most dangerous, Redman thought. He was thickset with clumsy hands and the coarse features of a peasant. He was also carrying the machine-pistol.

Engage him in conversation, Redman wondered? Get

him close enough to trip him over? But then what? With the other man Subhi nearby, and with the helicopter blocking the exit from the clearing, what hope was there?

Squatting down in front of Debbie, Fawaz offered to place a lighted cigarette between her lips.

'No thank you.'

Redman saw her swallow, saw how she forced a smile.

Fawaz became more attentive. He sat down in front of her.

To the west the sun was low, dipping out beneath the cloud, a hazy, pink blur of light behind some trees at the edge of the clearing. Redman watched the shadows crawl across to the truck, counting the minutes that Khatib had been away, wondering if Debbie had somehow managed to free her hands and what use it would be if she had.

He'd all but given up trying to free his own hands by the time Khatib returned.

The tall man approached Redman directly.

'I understand you are acquainted with a Mr Owen Mitchell,' Khatib said. 'I require his address in Brisbane.'

'Look in the phone book.' Redman started sweating.

'Mr Redman, I am in a hurry. There are seven Mitchells with the initial O in the directory. I suggest you answer me so we may conclude our business without unpleasantness.'

Redman's silence was a mistake.

Khatib nodded to Fawaz who immediately slipped a hand inside Debbie's blouse.

She became rigid – then cried out in pain.

'OK, OK.' Using his forearm as a lever, Redman strained against the cord until his wrist was slippery with blood.

'Well?' Khatib was waiting.

'147 Burnside Avenue.' Redman spat the words out. 'Get that bastard away from her.'

Khatib opened the door of the Trooper, shuffling through the glass on the floor with his foot.

Now, Redman thought. The bullet comes now. He was calm, as though he was observing himself from somewhere else.

Since Fawaz had moved away from Debbie she too had become calm again, leaning back against the wheel with her eyes partly closed.

'Further instructions are being transmitted to me,' Khatib said. 'Until I receive them you will remain under guard.'

'Then what?' Redman unclenched his teeth.

'There is a saying in my country: bees that have honey in their mouths have stings in their tails.' Khatib smiled. 'I think perhaps you have only tasted the honey, Mr Redman. Goodbye.'

Across the clearing the shadows had grown longer. Redman watched Khatib and Subhi pass through them, walking through alternate bands of light and dark, through a pale-pink sunset as unreal as everything else that had happened today. The helicopter too was pink, illuminated in the rays of a sun obscured by atmospheric dust rising from the far-off valley.

The Hughes took off slowly, hovering for several seconds before it climbed above the trees and swung away to the south-west.

Reprieve, Redman thought. But for how long?

'Steven,' Debbie whispered.

He swivelled round so he could see her properly. Her expression told him she was trying to convey a message.

Fawaz came to talk to her. 'You have food in your truck?' he asked.

'I can open some cans,' she said. 'We have coffee as well.'

'You think you are smart, yes? Because you are a girl you believe I will allow you to do what you wish.'

'Don't you like girls?' There was a mocking smile on Debbie's lips. 'Is that why you hurt me just now?'

'You know nothing.'

'You like boys, don't you?' she said. 'You enjoyed finding out if my friend is circumcised, I could see you did.'

Redman held his breath. She was challenging Fawaz, deliberately provoking him.

'I show you what I like.' Fawaz knelt down and unzipped Debbie's jeans.

She sat unprotesting while he forced her legs apart and thrust his hands between her thighs.

'Wait a second.' Debbie leaned forwards and whispered something to him.

'Ah.' Fawaz grinned. 'I shall watch you.' He reached behind her to untie the cord.

In the half light Redman saw her hands go to her hair. She ran her fingers through it, combing out the sand from her pony-tail, keeping one hand behind her neck.

'I take you now.' Unholstering his machine-pistol, Fawaz began to stand up.

A second later he was screaming.

From the socket of his left eye protruded a four-inch sliver of glass. He screamed again, reeling backwards as Debbie kicked him in the throat and ripped the pistol from his grasp.

She shot him twice at a range of less than eighteen inches, once in the stomach and once in the head.

Redman watched in disbelief, stunned by her ferocity and by the chilling way she'd handled the gun. But now it was over she seemed dazed, uncertain of where she was.

He called her name.

Pulling up her zip she started to come towards him but collapsed against the side of the truck, overtaken by spasms of vomiting.

When at length she was able to sit down and untie the cord from his wrists, Redman could feel her shaking. He stayed leaning against the wheel, holding her in his arms until she had recovered.

'We have to move,' he said.

She shivered. 'They won't come back in the dark, will they?'

'We're not going to take the chance.' He saw her palm was bleeding.

'It was the glass.' She wiped her hand on her blouse. 'I couldn't grip it properly – it was all tangled up in my hair when I tried to get it out.'

He looked at her. 'You take a lot of getting used to. You know that, don't you? What the hell did you say to Fawaz?'

'I told him I needed to go to the bathroom.'

Redman tore a sleeve off his shirt, bandaging Debbie's hand with half of it before wrapping the other half around his damaged wrist.

'Walking wounded,' she said. 'Is your head all right? You've got an awful bruise.'

'It's OK.' He went to see if the Trooper's headlights worked. Debbie followed him, skirting around the body of Fawaz in order to avoid stepping over it.

'Perhaps he killed Jennifer Decker,' she said.

'Eye for an eye? Is that what you mean?'

'I didn't mean anything.'

He switched on the headlights. In the beams he could pick out the flat area of sand where the Hughes had landed. Beyond it the road disappeared into the darkness on the far side of the clearing.

'Coen,' he said. 'We'll have to get there tonight. Or carry on down to Laura and see if we can find a motel. I have to phone Owen.'

Debbie climbed into the truck. 'You didn't have to give Owen's address to Khatib,' she said.

'I didn't give it to him. That wasn't Owen's address.'

She sat in silence, waiting until the truck was underway before she spoke again. 'So what now?' she asked.

Redman had been waiting for the question. 'We're pulling out,' he said, 'once I've got hold of Owen and we've found some way to dump the Trooper. It's no good pretending we can handle this by ourselves. Not anymore. IMT are just a part of it, part of something bigger than we could ever handle. We're already in so far over our heads that if we're not careful we won't get out of it. Someone else has to be told what's going on.'

'Like who?'

Redman wrenched at the steering-wheel. 'How does the US Ambassador sound? I'll catch a plane to Canberra as soon as we get to Cairns. Let's see what the Pentagon has to say about Mr Nassim Khatib and his goddamn Omega Project.'

'What about us, then? You and me.'

He took his eyes off the road long enough to glance at her. 'Do you remember a conversation we had about that a couple of hundred years ago?'

'About living happily ever after?'

'Do you want to try?'

'I don't see how we can. The US Government aren't going to believe you. They'll probably have you arrested. We haven't any photos. Khatib took the film.'

'Look in the glove-compartment.' Redman had seen the canister the moment he'd got back in the truck.

She inspected the film with amazement. 'This is crazy,' she said. 'I saw Khatib take it.'

'So did I. Or I thought I did. Either he left it there or he put it back – after he'd been talking over his radio.'

'Why would he do that?'

Redman shrugged. 'To get rid of it – the same way he was going to get rid of us. He was probably planning to burn the truck. The film wasn't any more important to him than we were.'

'Why not throw it away, then?'

'I don't know. It's like everything else we don't know.'

'Not everything,' she said. 'ABE stands for airburst experiment and GE means groundburst experiment. We know that now, don't we?'

'Sure. What difference does that make? What about the

second airburst experiment in the Solomons? Why didn't Khatib mention it? Who the hell's running this Consortium? Who did Khatib speak to on the radio?' He paused. 'The real crazy thing is that after all this, after damn nearly getting blown to pieces, we haven't the faintest idea what's going on.'

'They're bomb tests,' Debbie said. 'Owen's wrong. I don't care what he thinks. This is a new kind of bomb – a superbomb. We saw it today. A whole valley full of flame.'

'Yeah.' There was little doubt in Redman's mind either. There hadn't been for days, particularly not since this morning when one thought more than any other had begun to haunt him. He could still remember Owen reading from the book, remember how his voice had gone flat when he described the Japanese reaction to the Hiroshima explosion. But there had been a reason for Hiroshima, Redman thought. Today there was no reason, nothing to explain who was doing the testing, what the tests were for and why they were being carried out in the Pacific. Nor was there an answer to a more disturbing question.

He drove automatically, allowing his concentration to lapse on the straights where the headlights made it easy to see the ruts so he could think about the puzzle for the last time before he handed it over to someone, else to solve.

Perhaps there was more than one puzzle, he thought. Is that what Khatib had meant? Was it just possible for a bee that had honey in its mouth to have more than one sting in its tail?

Seven

'Look, I am sorry about this.' The secretary refilled Redman's cup with coffee. 'I don't know what the Ambassador's doing in there.'

'It's OK,' he said.

'Mr Washburn isn't usually like this. I'll give him another five minutes, then I'll buzz him.'

Redman watched her bustle away. She was an irritating woman who wouldn't leave him alone. In the last hour she'd fussed about with magazines, commented on his bruise and continually asked if there was anyone he needed to telephone to say he'd been delayed. As a result he was relieved when she came back to say the US Ambassador was ready to see him now.

'That door there.' She pointed. 'You can go right in.'

Seated at the far end of a glass-topped table were three men. One of them stood up.

'Mr Redman.' He offered his hand. 'I'm Thomas Washburn. This is Colonel Corliss and Commander Slater. They've travelled here to Canberra overnight to attend this meeting.'

Redman glanced at Corliss briefy, remembering Hawthorne's phone call about the visit from the FAA. He shook hands with Slater first, an elderly man with a lined face and thick, bushy eyebrows. Corliss was younger, one of the FAA's hard-bitten professionals, Redman thought. A career man who believed expensive suits were a sign of authority.

'Please sit down.' Washburn remained on his feet. 'I expect you're surprised to find the Commander and Colonel Corliss here.'

'I know Colonel Corliss works for the FAA. Hawthorne told me he'd been at Airtech. Look, maybe there are some wires crossed here. I haven't come to talk about an aircraft going down in the Solomons.'

'I understand. Your telephone call made that perfectly clear. But I'm afraid it's because of your call that other people have to be involved.' Washburn looked awkward. 'Mr Redman, as an American citizen you're entitled to the full assistance of this embassy. Let me assure you that nothing you hear this morning will prejudice your rights in any way. But you must appreciate there are occasionally times when the rights of an individual may be subordinated in the national interest of the United States.'

'And this is one of those times?' Redman carefully placed his envelope on the table in front of him.

'Yes it is. Colonel Corliss will explain. He and Commander Slater will speak to you alone. If you'd like to see me before you leave, please ask my secretary. You're also welcome to phone me again at any time.' Washburn nodded at the others before walking quickly from the room.

'OK.' Corliss removed his jacket. 'Let's get this going, shall we? First of all you can forget the FAA. I work for the National Security Council in Washington. The Commander's from British Intelligence. He represents the interests of the UK Government. Do you have a problem with any of that, Redman?'

'No.' Redman's unease had been replaced by apprehension.

'You're here to tell us some mad bastard is running round the South Pacific letting off bombs – right?' Corliss was trying to stare Redman down. 'And you've brought some pictures to show us so we won't think you're full of shit.'

Redman decided not to say anything.

'Let me spell it out for you,' Corliss said. 'In the eyes of the US Government you're a loose cannon. You can do two things with a loose cannon. Tip it overboard so it doesn't cause any more damage or tie it up with a rope and make it work for you. Now, because I can tip you overboard any time I want, if you don't want to drown, you'd better listen good. Have you got that, Redman?'

Redman knew he had miscalculated badly. The ground rules were all wrong. This was no meeting to discuss his photographs.

'I'm listening,' he said quietly.

Corliss lit a cigarette. 'A couple of years ago the US Government was approached by three Middle-East countries: Syria, Egypt and Jordan. They wanted to do a deal – a deal to get them in a position to do business with Israel on level terms. What they had in mind was the acquisition of nuclear capability. I guess they figured if Iraq could do it, they could do it. Because they'd had enough of Israel being the only nuclear power in the region, they told the US they didn't give a shit about the Nuclear Non-proliferation Treaty. What these guys wanted was a stick to wave around that's as big as the one Israel's got.'

'I don't understand,' Redman said. 'I thought no one knew whether Israel had nuclear arms or not.'

'Have you heard of a guy called Vanunu? Mordechai Vanunu.'

'I don't think so.'

'Between 1976 and 1985 Vanunu worked as a technician for the Israeli Nuclear Research Centre at Dimona out in the middle of the Negev Desert. In January 1986 he took fifty-seven photographs and a whole lot of classified information to a journalist called Peter Hounam in Sydney. Hounam flew him to London in secret to be interviewed by the British. The Brits turned Vanunu inside out and spent four months analysing his data. Then, on the 30th of September he was lured to Rome and kidnapped by MOSSAD, the Israeli secret service. The Israelis tried him for treason and aggravated espionage. They threw him in jail for eighteen years. Vanunu stuffed up Israel's security. It's not only the West who think the Israelis have developed nuclear weapons. Syria, Egypt and Jordan know damn well they have.'

Slater coughed to indicate he wanted to say something. 'It may not be that simple,' he said. 'British Intelligence believe it's quite possible the Israelis deliberately used Vanunu to leak information to the West – because it's in Israel's interest for the world to think they have a nuclear weapon stockpile. In any event, now you know why the COAS approached the US.'

'Is the COAS the Consortium?' Redman asked.

'Right.' Corliss nodded. 'Consortium of Arab States, three countries who don't like the idea of Israel having a finger on a nuclear trigger. The Arabs figured that after the Gulf War the US might not like it much either. So they came up with this deal.'

'For the US to help them develop a nuclear bomb?' Redman said.

'They weren't that stupid. They knew damn well the US wouldn't even think about it. But what they did know is that the US is real keen on trying to stabilize the mess in the Middle-East to safeguard oil supplies. The Arabs decided we'd listen to anything which might force the Israelis to start talking about the Palestinians, the problem in the occupied territories and every other damn thing.'

Slater was leaning back in his chair studying Redman. 'How do you think the Middle East might be stabilized?' he said.

Redman shrugged. 'I don't know.'

'I'll tell you,' Slater said. 'The best way is to copy history – use what's worked before. In any part of the world where there's a potential for conflict, if you make sure no one's more powerful than anyone else, you get a strategic stand-off. The politicians call it Mutually Assured Destruction – MAD to you. It worked for fifty years between NATO and the old Warsaw-pact countries.'

'What stand-off?' Redman said. 'If the Arabs knew the US wouldn't help them develop nuclear weapons, what did they want?' The answer was staring him in the face, he thought, and he'd never once considered it.

Corliss stubbed out his cigarette and lit another. 'They gave us a choice. Either they'd start their own nuclear development programme using enriched plutonium and technical assistance from China and India, or the US could help them develop something else altogether – a non-nuclear weapon that had certain tactical disadvantages but one that would scare the living shit out of the Israelis.'

Redman was more relieved than surprised. In the back of his mind he'd always imagined it would be something like this.

Slater was still looking at him. 'You must have had some idea of what was going on,' he said. 'Surely.'

'I've been kind of busy.' Redman was careful not to over-react. 'Trying to keep alive.'

Corliss smiled slightly. 'You've been in the wrong place at the wrong time ever since you set foot in the Solomons.'

'What does that mean?'

'It means it's not only the US and the UK who aren't about to let you screw up this project. Project Omega has three partners: the US, the British and the Consortium of Arab States. It's not just us who've been trying to reel you in.'

'What's it got to do with the British?' Redman glanced

at Slater. 'Why are British companies like IMT working on this thing?'

'IMT are a convenience,' Slater said. 'So are Consolidated Metals. British companies have a long association with the Middle East. You probably recall all the trouble after the Gulf War when UK manufacturers were implicated in the development of Saddam Hussein's long-range gun.'

'And the British use Middle East oil,' Redman said. 'Surprise.'

Slater frowned. 'We're involved in Project Omega because of our expertise in fuel-air bombs and because that expertise translates directly into the development of dust types and dust dispersal methods for large-scale non-nuclear explosions. But I don't much care to answer your questions, Redman. All you need to know is that Project Omega has been established to produce what appears, at face value, to be an Arab weapon system having a destructive potential at least as great as a medium-sized nuclear device. If you don't like that, or if you're unhappy with the idea of British participation, I suggest you keep quiet about it.'

'You didn't miss what Commander Slater just said, did you?' Corliss blew out a stream of cigarette smoke.

Redman hadn't missed it. 'So the UK has handed the Arabs all the technology they need to make a new kind of bomb that looks good,' he said. 'But one they can't use strategically because it's too hard to deliver to a target.'

Corliss smiled again. 'Except of course the Israelis won't know how strategically dangerous it might be or might not be. All they'll know is that somehow or other Syria, Egypt and Jordan have got their hands on a non-nuclear, non-biological and non-chemical superbomb.'

'How are the Israelis supposed to know that?'

'Because the US is going to tell them,' Corliss said. 'And because not long from now there are going to be three official desert tests in the Middle East. Big ones. No one's going to miss those. The US part of the deal is to leak intelligence data to Israel beforehand. Israel will try to monitor the explosions, photograph them and do everything but taste them. We'll just make sure they don't get too close.'

'Why mess about in the South Pacific, then?' The answer came to Redman before he'd finished speaking.

'Development,' said Slater. 'The technology has to be as efficient as we can make it. The airburst experiment in the Solomons was designed to check out the optimum dust concentration levels, and the groundburst experiment was a full-scale explosion to make certain the three desert tests will look as impressive as possible.'

'One experiment in the Solomons,' Redman said. 'And another on Cape York. Two experiments.'

Slater nodded. 'As things have turned out, we could have probably managed with one. They've been more successful than anyone expected them to be.'

'Why Malaita and Cape York?'

'Why do you think?' Corliss was impatient. 'The Arabs didn't want to experiment in their own backyards. Israeli intelligence is pretty damn good. They didn't want Israel getting any advance notice. That's why the Consortium has been hung up about the weather conditions out here. Israel has access to French satellite data. The whole project relies on secrecy.' He looked directly at Redman. 'So you can imagine how pleased we were when you phoned Washburn from Cairns. You saved us a lot of trouble.'

Redman returned the stare. 'Pleased because I'm not a security problem anymore? So you can shut me up like you shut up Jennifer Decker? For Christ's sake, she didn't know anything. You didn't have to kill her.'

'I didn't say we did.' Corliss stubbed out his cigarette. 'I've told you. The project has three partners. The British are supplying technical support. The US are responsible for leading the Israelis along by their noses, but it's the

Consortium who are doing the work. It's their bomb, not ours. If you want to get excited about Jennifer Decker, talk to them.'

'Khatib,' Redman said. 'Jesus. And you think I'm a loose cannon. Where did the Arabs find him?'

'He's Syrian,' Slater said. 'An unstable, politically-motivated terrorist with a degree from Oxford University in England. He's anti-Zionist, anti-Israel and tends to take matters into his own hands. The Arabs have been worried about him for months. Unfortunately they don't seem to be able to control what he does anymore than we can.'

'Well, someone'd better start.' Redman's anger was beginning to surface. 'Do you guys think you're God or something?'

Corliss stood up. 'I'll tell you what we think. We think Project Omega is in trouble. And we think you're going to fix it for us.'

'I don't care about your goddamn project. Fix it yourself.'

'You don't get it yet, do you?' Corliss leaned across the table. 'This isn't a game, Redman. This is how things work in the real world. Do you honestly believe you outsmarted Khatib on the peninsula?'

Redman's anger died. He said nothing, waiting for whatever was coming next.

'The Israelis don't sit around on their arses, either,' Corliss said. 'They watch everything, everyone, every-where. A month ago they had people in Hong Kong asking questions about IMT. Before that they broke into a warehouse in Sydney where the dust was being stored. Israel has to have guessed the Consortium is experimen-ting with explosive dust. What they don't know is how dangerous a dust bomb could be in the right hands.'

'Or the wrong hands.' Slater interrupted. 'The Israelis need to find out if the Arab development is as big a threat to their national security as they think it is.'

'Which is where you come in, Redman.' Corliss was still

on his feet. 'You're going to confirm Project Omega is the worst thing that's ever happened to the State of Israel – persuade the Israelis to take a good look at the desert tests so they can see what a nice big dust explosion could do to Tel Aviv or Haifa.'

'Why the hell should I?'

Corliss smiled. 'Did you have a look inside a Solomon Island jail while you were there? The Honiara police have these natives who swear they saw you push Mrs Decker overboard into some crocodile-infested estuary off the Malaita coast. Tough break for her. Bad luck for you.'

Redman stood up from his chair. 'Bullshit,' he said. 'You wouldn't risk the publicity.'

'Right,' Corliss agreed. 'Which is why you'd never make it to trial. Let's talk about what you're actually going to do, shall we? I'll explain something to you, then I'll ask you a question.'

'What?'

'Three days ago when Khatib contacted us, he was instructed to let you keep your film, and then make you and your pretty girlfriend believe you'd managed to escape by your own efforts. Now, why would we want to go to all that trouble?'

Redman's brain was into overload. He was bewildered, struggling to make sense out of what Corliss had said. 'Why?' he muttered.

'The girl believes you got away by killing one of Khatib's men, doesn't she?'

Redman nodded.

'And she saw the explosion in the valley?'

He nodded again.

Taking Redman's envelope, Corliss emptied the contents on to the table. There were fourteen photographs in all. Six of them were of the ships, the beach and of the pylon with the truck parked beneath it. A further five showed the AT 302s at work above the dust-cloud emerging from the pylon. The remaining three photographs were more dramatic; shots of an eerie red valley, of a floodlit sky and a part frame of the valley-mouth engulfed in flame.

'Not bad.' Corliss left the photos on the table. 'I've an interesting picture too.'

From his brief-case he withdrew a photographic print. He placed it face down in front of Redman. 'If you've been wondering how we're going to use you as a pipeline into the Israeli intelligence network, that might give you an idea.'

Confronted by the unthinkable, Redman couldn't lift his hands from the tabletop.

'Go ahead.' Corliss slid the photograph closer.

Redman flipped it over, knowing what he was going to find.

The picture was very sharp. Sharp enough for him to see the flecks of colour in Debbie's eyes and pick out the tiny blemish at the corner of her mouth.

'Nice picture,' Corliss said. 'Makes you want to take her to bed, doesn't it? The guy who took it thought it was great. He's got a print stuck on his office wall.'

Inside Redman's head, a million thoughts began to rearrange themselves. He was dazed, incapable of hearing what Corliss was saying to him now.

'IDF,' Corliss repeated.

'What?'

'Israeli Defence Force.'

'Jesus.' Redman slumped into a chair. 'Jesus Christ. She couldn't be.'

Corliss raised his eyebrows. Then he grinned. 'Well, how about that. You lucky son of a bitch. She's been letting you screw her, hasn't she?'

'Mind your own goddamn business.' Redman threw the photograph across the room. 'Who is she?'

'Melissa Sarid. She works out of Beirut for the reconnaissance division of the Sayerat Golani. That's part

of the IDF. We think she was following Khatib when he
came to Australia three months ago. She must have tripped
over you after Jennifer Decker started shooting her mouth
off to the newspapers.'

A section of Redman's mind was working indepen-
dently – recalling the way she'd triggered the bomb inside
his house, how she'd frozen when first he'd tried to kiss
her and, more than anything, remembering the cold-
blooded execution of Fawaz in the clearing. He felt numb,
unable to believe she had betrayed him like this. She was
someone else, he thought bitterly. A stranger who cared
less for him than for a job she was paid to do.

'Pay-back time.' Corliss's voice cut through his thoughts.
'Now you can give it to her like she gave it to you.'

'You want me to feed her information,' Redman said
slowly. 'Don't you? For her to give to Israeli Intelligence.
Do you expect me to do that? Now I know who she is?'

'You'll do what you have to do.' Corliss gathered up the
photographs and put them back into the envelope. 'Here.'
He tossed the envelope across the table. 'Make sure she
gets her own copies for the IDF. That ought to start them
worrying.'

'She knows they're dust explosions.' The rest of Redman's brain was beginning to function again. 'She'll have
already told someone.'

'So what. She's seen what a valley full of the stuff can do.
Your job's to convince her that Khatib and his Consortium
can do the same thing in down-town Tel Aviv.'

'But they can't,' Redman said.

'Look, I've told you. The Israelis don't know that. As
soon as we give them our satellite pictures of the desert
tests and they put them together with their own information, Israel's going to get real jumpy.' Corliss lit another
cigarette. 'And once that happens they'll start talking with
the Arabs. Then we can go home, and the Pentagon can go
back to sleep.'

'Suppose I won't do it?' Redman said.

'Oh, you'll do it all right. Think of America while you're fucking her. Think how you'll be contributing to peace in the Middle East. You don't have a choice, Redman. Fall over on this, and you're history.'

Slater walked across the room to collect the photograph of Debbie. 'Do you have any questions before you go?' he asked.

Redman shook his head. 'The Australian police might get in the way,' he said. 'They're looking for me.'

'No, they're not,' Slater said. 'That's taken care of. So is the write-off of the vehicle you left in a ditch up in Queensland. You worry about your girlfriend – we'll worry about everything else. Telephone the embassy here every three days to keep in touch.' He put out his hand. 'Goodbye, Redman.'

He ignored the hand. 'You're no better than Khatib,' he said. 'You're sick, both of you.'

'The whole world's sick,' Corliss grunted. 'Don't let it get you down. Just do what you're told.' He went to open the door. 'Khatib left a message for you. I don't know what it means, but he said you would.'

Redman walked out into the corridor before he turned round. 'What message?'

'He sends his regards to Miss Sarid and says he hopes you enjoy sucking out all that honey.'

During the drive from the airport the rain had steadily become heavier. Outside the building it was bouncing off the sidewalk, and streaming off the awning over the front door in a waterfall.

Redman gave the taxi-driver thirty dollars.

'No, that's OK.' He didn't want the change.

Still standing in the rain, he checked to see if the lights were on in the apartment then looked for Owen's car. It was parked on the other side of the street behind a van. In front of the van stood Debbie's red Toyota. Except it wasn't Debbie's red Toyota, Redman thought. It was Melissa's.

Now he was here, he wasn't sure he could go in. How was he going to do this in front of Owen? he wondered. Maintaining a pretence in front of him would be about as easy as making Debbie believe the visit to Canberra had been a waste of time.

For a while he sheltered from the rain beneath the awning, not yet ready to trust himself. On the plane, to begin with, he'd been able to pretend this was something he could handle. But towards the end of the flight, the bitterness had been replaced by a different feeling – something he recognized at once – a familiar coldness that had made it possible to live with the memory of Josie, a leaching away of emotion so the hurt could never become too great.

Ignoring it, he shook off the rain and went into the lobby. To gain more time, instead of taking the elevator he climbed the stairs to the fifth floor, approaching Owen's door directly, but hesitating before he pushed the buzzer.

The delay was fatal. The longer he stood outside, the worse it got. Not coldness, but resentment – a rising anger that she had lied to him so thoroughly.

Ramming down the button as hard as he could, Redman held it down until the door opened.

'Oh, Steven.' Debbie stepped towards him. 'Thank God you're here. I've been so worried.'

She was barefoot, standing in the entrance with the light from the hallway shining through her hair. Her eyes were smiling at him.

Redman couldn't stand it. He hit her flat-handed round the face, driving her back into the apartment.

Before she could regain her balance he pushed her, then pushed her again.

'Stop it.' She stumbled backwards. 'Steven, stop it.'

He continued shoving until they reached the lounge where Redman threw her down on the sofa, disgusted as much with himself as he had been by the falseness of her greeting.

'Don't say anything,' he said. 'Not a thing. Just tell me where Owen is.'

She tried to pull down her skirt.

'Owen,' Redman said. 'Is he here?'

'Owen's dead.'

A paralysis spread upwards from his feet. Even after it had passed it was some seconds before he was sufficiently controlled to speak.

'When?' he said.

'Two days ago. I was trying to tell you but you wouldn't let me. It was a hit and run – outside the university. He died on the way to hospital.'

'It was murder.' Redman's expression was grim. 'Because of me. And because of you. Because of your precious Israeli Defence Force. Jesus Christ, I hope you burn in hell for this. Are you satisfied now? If I'd known who you were and what was going on I could have stopped this from happening.'

'Don't.' She covered her face. 'That's not true.'

'Damn you.' Redman prised her hands away. 'Look at me.'

She was crying. 'It's not what you think,' she whispered. 'You don't understand.'

'Oh yes I do. Two guys at the embassy spent four hours telling me who you are and what you do. I understand exactly. I wish to God I didn't.'

'You have to let me explain. You owe me that much. Please.' She spoke through her tears.

'I don't owe you anything.'

'That night at the restaurant,' she said. 'When you thought I didn't want to kiss you. It was because I knew this would happen to us. Don't you see, I didn't want to fall in love with you.'

'But you forced yourself – right? You pretended, so I'd take you up to the Cape. So you could get what you wanted.' He paused. 'For, who is it? the Sayerat Golani, your goddamn IDF. Well, Miss Sarid, I hope you enjoyed the ride. At least you didn't have to look at me when we made love. Lie back in the dark and do it for Israel. You're no better than a cheap whore.'

'I'm not a whore. Don't you ever, ever call me that.'

The tears suddenly stopped. Her eyes were flashing now, telling Redman there was a limit beyond which she would not let him go.

'OK, OK,' he said. 'You're not a whore. You just got carried away with your job. Tough business to be in.'

'I'll tell you who Debbie Hinton is, shall I?' She was shaking. 'If you really want to know why I couldn't make love with you unless it was dark, I'll tell you.'

'Don't bother.' His anger drained out of him. 'I don't want to hear it.'

She stood up. 'It's never crossed your mind how I might feel, has it? You're so obsessed with your dead wife and whatever it is you've found out at the embassy, you can't see any further than what you think is the truth – what you want to believe. Well, this is true as well.'

Turning her back on him she unbuttoned her blouse then reached up behind her to unfasten her brassiere.

'What the hell are you doing?' He watched with discomfort as she stripped to the waist and slid her skirt down over her hips. But when she swivelled round Redmond didn't know how to look.

Extending downwards from her throat, her body was disfigured with a network of crudely executed tattoos. Scrawled across her breasts were the words Jewish Whore. They were overlapped with Islamic crescents, swastikas and misspelt obscenities that seemed to have been written by a child.

He was too shocked to say anything at all.

'What's the matter?' She slipped her blouse back on. 'Don't you hate me enough to be pleased I look like this?'

Redman went to Owen's cupboard, returning with an unopened bottle of bourbon and the largest glass he could find.

He poured a drink automatically, numb again, thinking first of Owen, then of Jennifer Decker, of Warren Decker, of Josie and finally of Debbie Hinton – a girl who existed only in his mind.

'OK,' he said. 'If you want to tell me about it, I'm listening.'

She sat down beside him on the sofa. 'After my parents were divorced, my mother went back to live in Lebanon – to a market town called Nabatiya. She was there in 1983 when an Israeli convoy tried to drive through a crowd of Shiite Muslims who were celebrating Ashura. That's a holiday to commemorate the martyrdom of Muhammed's grandson, Hussein. The Shiites rioted. They attacked the Israeli soldiers with anything they could lay their hands on – guns, stones, grenades – even with their bare hands. It was the start of the whole disintegration of South Lebanon. You may have read about it.'

'No.' Redman shook his head.

'In 1986 my sister and I went to Nabatiya to visit our mother on her birthday. It was October 16th, the anniversary of the Ashura riot three years before. There was a lot of tension and some shooting in the streets. In the afternoon the Shiite Militia started killing anyone they suspected of being Jewish. Four men broke into the building where my mother lived. They were teenagers with Kalashnikovs. They raped my sister, my mother and then they raped me. I was eighteen years old.' She stopped talking.

'Go on,' Redman said. 'Finish it.'

'When they'd done what they wanted to do they threw my mother and my sister out of a window on the seventh floor and used them for target practice as they fell. I was much luckier. After they'd mutilated me with bits of broken milk bottle they squeezed ink from ball-point pens into the cuts for fun.'

Redman was drinking steadily, watching her face while she described the indescribable. She'd spoken calmly, in a matter-of-fact way as though she'd been talking about someone else.

'The IDF recruited me just over a year after it happened,' she said. 'There was a psychoanalyst in Haifa who thought working for the IDF would be a good idea. I don't expect you to feel sorry for me but I won't allow you to believe I made love to you because of my job. A lot of doctors said I'd never be able to make love to anyone. Until I met you I thought so too. Whatever you think, whatever you say, you can't ever take that away from me.'

Redman was confused by his reaction to what she'd told him. 'You didn't say who Debbie Hinton is.'

'Was. She's dead. Debbie was my sister. She was married to an American soldier – a nice guy called Geoff Hinton. He lives in Seattle. I write to him sometimes.'

'But you've never worked for WPA, have you? That was all garbage. The information you got about IMT and Consolidated Metals came from the people you work for. You even knew who Khatib was. That's why you asked me to describe the tall man from the launch on Malaita.'

She nodded. 'That doesn't mean I lied about my feelings for you. I just had to keep that part of me separate from what I did for the IDF. The Sayerat Golani had been following Khatib for eighteen months. There was a tip-off from Jordan saying that he was somehow involved in the development of a new Arab weapon system. But we didn't know what – not until you and I met each other.' She picked up Redman's glass and swallowed some bourbon. 'The embassy's told you what this is all about, haven't they?'

'Some of it.'

'But you won't tell me? Not now I've explained.'

'I wouldn't tell you the time. You could've explained before. But I guess that would've spoilt things for you.'

'I was too scared to explain. In case this happened.'

'Well, from here on you'd better be careful asking me for information. You see, I've got this nice new job. You're only supposed to hear what I want you to hear.' Redman took the glass away from her. 'You know, the funny thing is, right up until I got to the apartment, I thought I could do it – so one day you'd find out I wasn't as stupid as you thought I was. Crazy, isn't it?'

'Don't you believe what I've told you?'

'It doesn't matter one way or the other. Debbie Hinton doesn't exist. You did too good a job making me believe in your sister. I'd liked to have met her.'

She stood up from the sofa, her eyes on his face. 'You can't forget about us.'

'You want to bet? Go and find someone else.'

'I don't want anyone else. I want you. I want you more than anything I've ever wanted in my life.' She began to reach out to touch him but stopped herself. 'I'll do anything you ask me to do. I'll go anywhere with you.'

'To get information?'

Her eyes clouded over. 'Don't do this to me – please.'

'Khatib knew you better than I did. He knew what would happen on the peninsula. He let it happen. I'd trust him further than I'd trust you.' Redman gave her the envelope of photographs. 'You can keep these – if you haven't already got your own copies.'

'You're wrong about me. For God's sake why won't you understand? I've told you the truth. I was supposed to interview you, ask about Khatib, ask about what you did in the Solomons. That doesn't mean what happened afterwards between us was a lie. You can't believe that.'

'I believe what one of the guys in Canberra told me. He said the world's sick.' Redman hesitated. 'Look, I'm sorry it's turned out this way, but I'm not about to make any more mistakes. Do what you have to do. I don't want any part of it, or any part of you.'

She started to reply, but changed her mind. 'This came.' She handed him an envelope. 'I found it this evening when I let myself in. It's addressed to you care of Owen Mitchell.'

Redman recognized the handwriting. It was a letter, a single sheet of paper wih Owen's signature at the bottom.

'Who's it from?' she asked.

'Owen. To say his apartment was broken into while we were away. He wanted us to know that whoever it was must have seen his notes on the dust analysis. They were right here in the lounge.'

Redman carried on reading. 'It sounds as though he got scared after he'd played back the message we left on his answering machine.'

'That's why he used the mail,' she said. 'Just in case something happened to him. What else does it say?'

'Didn't you steam it open before I got here?'

'No.' She flushed. 'I've been at the Hilton. You promised to call me there, remember? I left three more messages on Owen's machine telling him to be careful. They'll still be on the tape if you don't believe me. I only came here this evening because I was so worried about you and because I heard about Owen's accident. I thought you might come straight to the apartment.'

'Been better if you'd stayed at your hotel, wouldn't it? Christ, what a mess. Owen's notes killed him. Khatib's got the answer from the notes that he tried to get from us.'

'What answer? What do you mean?'

'Figure it out for yourself. Ask the clever people you work for.' Redman glanced at her. 'Listen, you're in trouble. Khatib's going to come after you – just like the bastard's going to come after me. You'd better find somewhere safe.'

'What about you?' This time she did touch him.

Redman felt her hand warm upon his arm. 'I'm going to live happily ever after,' he said. 'But not with you.' He reached into his pocket for the *nguzunguzu* and gave the little carving to her. 'You keep this,' he said. 'I don't want it anymore.'

She removed her hand. 'Is that all you have to say to me?'

He nodded. 'I'll see you around.'

Wordlessly she turned to go.

Redman didn't say goodbye. Instead, unable to watch her walk away, and too bitter to consider the consequences of what he had done tonight, he picked up the bourbon bottle and carried it with him into the bedroom.

Outside the apartment block, the rain had turned to drizzle, affording the technician in the van a better look at the girl than he'd expected. He watched her walk to her car before he removed his headset and switched off the bank of tape-recorders. Although in a way he felt sorry for her because of what he'd overheard, his voice was free of sentiment when he lifted the phone and made his report to Corliss.

In the Timor Sea, on board the mother-ship of the COAS, a different, but equally disturbing report had already caused a change of plans. Now the Mitchell notes had made it clear that the second unauthorized Solomon Island test had not gone undetected, events were beginning to overtake Nassim Khatib. With the promise of real, uninhibited Arab power slipping from his grasp, and with the knowledge that the reward for individual effort was likely to be unpleasant, the time for emergency measures was overdue.

During the next twelve hours in Washington and on the bridge of the mother-ship, decisions would be made and, for a while, the future of Project Omega would depend as much on the ability of Corliss and Khatib to rectify mistakes as it would depend on the actions of men gathered in Jerusalem to discuss how great their own mistakes had been.

Eight

The last time he'd drunk too much of Owen's bourbon it had worked well enough. But tonight the effect was disappointing. Shortly before three in the morning Redman took the bottle into the bathroom and emptied what remained of its contents into the toilet.

Instead of deadness there was an edge to his mind. Because of it, over the last five hours, he had come to appreciate the true significance of the second Solomon Island experiment. He understood now that it had never been part of the authorized testing programme. It was a secret, a separate airburst experiment using enhanced dust to put the Consortium one step ahead of the US and the UK.

Studying himself in the mirror, Redman wondered how he could ever have been so stupid. There had been two puzzles after all, a project inside a project, a private Arab development programme that the West knew nothing about.

Everything was clear – the reason why Khatib's interrogation on the peninsula had centred on the second experiment, the need to silence Jennifer and the incredible ignorance of Corliss and Slater.

US and UK intelligence had never been a threat to the

Consortium, Redman realized. They had no idea what the Arabs were up to. On the peninsula, Khatib had been happy to co-operate with the West. But that was before the Consortium had learned about Owen's notes, before Owen had become the threat. Since then everything had changed. Now, to protect their secret, the COAS had two more loose ends to tie up – Melissa Sarid and Steven Redman – the only other people who were aware of the second test.

Redman knew he had a choice: tell Corliss the West was being double-crossed, or let someone else do it. Like someone from the IDF, he thought. Debbie could do it, he decided. As long as the Consortium didn't get to her first.

The danger to Debbie kept nagging at him, so much so, that for a while he considered calling her at the Hilton to repeat his warning. But would she be there? Was she already on her way back to Israel? If she wasn't, what was she doing now?

Gripping the bottle by the neck, he brought it down hard on the edge of the toilet bowl. The result was sufficiently satisfying to break the spell.

He remembered how Owen used to tell him that it was only the unlucky who got unluckier. But not forever, Redman thought. He'd damn near made it with Debbie. Although like Owen and like Josie she too was gone, the sooner he started concentrating on tomorrow, the quicker he'd forget her, and the quicker he did that, the more likely it was his luck would improve again.

Returning to the lounge he sat down at the table with pen and paper. By day-break his options had been reduced to three, and by nine o'clock when he left the apartment, the winner had emerged. As well as being pleased with his decision, he was anxious to get going so he could see how correct the guesses about himself would prove to be.

He took Owen's car, the little Ford with the cracked windshield, pushing north through the commuter traffic on a sunny Brisbane morning, only once allowing his thoughts to dwell on Debbie when he saw a red Toyota in his mirror. It turned off at an intersection before he made his first stop to buy the knife, and by the time he'd been to the bank and found somewhere to buy a body-belt, he was able to pretend the memories of her were already beginning to fade.

It was gone ten when he reached the office building. He went right in, anticipating the reaction from his secretary.

'Hi, Trixie.' Redman surprised her.

'Oh, good heavens.' She stood up quickly from her desk. 'I didn't think – I mean, I didn't –' She stopped talking, her cheeks red with embarrassment.

'I know you didn't.'

'The newspapers,' she said. 'Your house was bombed – and Mrs Decker – when you went to the Solomons. Why didn't you call me?'

'It's a bit complicated.'

She sat down again. 'Are you in trouble, Mr Redman?'

'No.' He smiled. 'It was just a mess. I suppose Hawthorne's been calling?'

'The whole world's been calling, not just Mr Hawthorne. I've had people here, too. They wanted to know where you were.'

'Colonel Corliss,' Redman said. 'And a guy called Slater?'

She nodded. 'I had two calls from someone yesterday asking if you were back yet. They wouldn't leave their name but I'm supposed to ring them back if you arrive – it's a Darwin number.'

Redman felt his skin crawl. Had Khatib diverted the ships to Darwin or had he sent a radio message to someone there? 'I have to fly to California,' he said. 'Today, or as soon as I can get on a flight.'

His secretary looked at him. 'I'm not sure you have a job there anymore – or here either come to that. Mr Hawthorne made me fax him all the quotes for the

Indonesian order and told me I was to run the office until someone else came to take over.'

'That's the nice thing about Airtech,' Redman said. 'Great employee relations. I'll talk Hawthorne round when I see him. Now, listen, I want you to go to the travel agent – don't phone them – get down there and stay there until they guarantee me a reservation. I'll go first-class if I have to. It's important. When you come back, send a fax to Airtech saying what time I'm getting in. Ask Hawthorne to have someone meet the flight in San Francisco. Say I'll explain everything when I arrive.'

'You'll have to collect the tickets from the airport. The agent won't issue them while I wait.'

'That's OK.' He opened the door to his office. 'Assuming I still work here, how about some coffee?'

She relaxed sufficiently to smile. 'You know, it's funny to have you back. I haven't been sure what was going to happen.'

'Me neither.' He went to sit down at his desk, waiting until she'd brought the coffee before he picked up the telephone and asked for international.

It took some time for the operator to find the number of the Tambea Village Resort and it was another two or three minutes before the hotel receptionist managed to locate Jimmy.

'Hi.' Redman was relieved to hear his voice. 'Jimmy, this is Steve Redman. I'm calling from Brisbane.'

'You track me down, eh? Like a good Indian. You are still in trouble?'

'Yeah,' Redman said. 'But maybe for not much longer. Look, there are a couple of things I'd like you to do for me. I'll be mailing you those photographs we took at the airstrip. I want you to give them to the police in Honiara and explain what happened while we were on Malaita. Someone's saying I murdered Mrs Decker by throwing her off the *Kwaibala*. I need you to tell the police what really went on there.'

'So you will send me the picture of Mrs Decker? The bad one?'

'Right. Until you get it, and until you hear from me again, you'd better be careful. Keep your head down. There's a whole lot of nasty things happening. If anyone besides the police start asking questions, tell them you don't know anything. Say you hired the boat for me, but nothing else.'

'OK. I understand. That is all?'

'Not quite.' Redman continued speaking for several minutes, remembering to repeat his warning before he hung up.

He finished his coffee, endeavouring to decide whether he should send the negatives of the Malaitan photographs to Washburn at the embassy, and wondering how much risk there would be in trying to find out where Owen's funeral was being held.

Trixie returned while he was writing a covering letter to Jimmy.

She put her head round the door. 'You're confirmed OK,' she said. 'They put a reservation straight through on the computer. You're on a Qantas flight tonight. Check-in at eight-thirty. I told them you'd pick up the tickets at the airport.'

'Thanks. It might be an idea to send the fax to Hawthorne right away, so it'll be on his desk when he gets in.'

'Mr Redman, do you know someone called Debbie Hinton?'

'Why?'

'When Colonel Corliss came here he kept on asking if she'd gone to the Solomon Islands with you.'

'No.' Redman said. 'I've never heard of her. What else did he want to know?'

'Nothing really.' She glanced at the bandage on his wrist and then at the bruise on his temple. 'I suppose you wouldn't tell me what's going on, would you?'

'You wouldn't believe me.'

'Will you be coming back to Australia?'

'I'll let you know.' He paused. 'Look, I've got a lot to do this afternoon. I might not see you before I leave. If it means anything, I'd like you to know you're the best damn secretary anyone could want. You're wasted working for a rat-shit company like Airtech.'

'Oh.' She lowered her eyes. 'Goodbye then.'

He gathered up his parcels from the desk. 'If you get any more calls from Darwin, tell them I've gone back to the States, but don't say when.'

Redman left her standing in the doorway. It was a lousy way to say goodbye, he thought. But not as lousy as the way he'd had to say goodbye to Debbie.

The woman at the Qantas desk was speaking to him.

'I'm sorry. What?' Redman had been watching a swarthy well-dressed man checking in at the next counter.

'Do you have any luggage, Mr Redman?'

'Only hand baggage.'

'OK.' She returned his passport with his boarding-pass. 'Gate three. Boarding at nine-forty-five. Have a nice flight.'

'Thanks.' He left the counter, searching among the crowd for inquisitive eyes while he went to mail his letter to Jimmy.

Despite being confident that no one had followed him this afternoon, he was ill at ease. It was conceivable Khatib could have guessed what he might do. And Owen's killer could have been told to stay on here in Brisbane. Just in case of the odd loose end.

He found the Air Nuigini office at the far end of the terminal. It was staffed by a pretty Melanesian girl with fuzzy hair.

'Can I see your ticket please?' she said.

'I haven't got one yet.' He smiled at her. 'I've just found

out I have to be in Papua New Guinea for a meeting first thing tomorrow. Is there any chance of getting on a flight tonight?'

'I'm sorry. I'm afraid not. There's one to Port Moresby tomorrow, but it leaves dreadfully early – at one-thirty in the morning. It's never very full, though.'

Redman breathed a sigh of relief. The idea of spending another night at Owen's apartment was unattractive. It would also be pushing his luck further than he wanted to push it.

He paid for the ticket in twenty-dollar bills, collecting some hotel brochures from the girl before he headed for the wash-room to put the balance of his cash back into his money-belt. Already he felt better. Step one, Redman thought. The hard one. Step two would be easier and, as long as Jimmy was successful, step three to Honiara would be a piece of cake.

Inside a cubicle in the wash-room he took off his money-belt. It contained nearly $4,000, all that remained of Josie's life-insurance payout and what little he'd managed to save from his salary over the last two years.

He was repacking the belt when his knife clattered on to the tiles. At the same time someone entered one of the other cubicles.

Redman picked up the knife quickly, hoping it hadn't been seen under the door. It was not the kind of knife to be carrying around an air terminal and the last thing he could afford was for some well-meaning passenger to report him.

Because he could find nowhere to leave it, he slipped the knife back under his belt and rebuttoned his shirt. Before he left the cubicle, he tore up the Qantas boarding-pass and flushed the pieces down the toilet.

Half-way to the wash-room something attracted his attention – shiny flecks on the wet tiles by the hand-basin – tiny, glittering silver flecks.

He was still turning round when the man burst out of the cubicle.

Redman hurled himself sideways. But he was already trapped. Trapped by the thin steel wire around his throat. He felt it tighten, felt it white hot, biting into his windpipe, choking off his breath.

Clawing at it with both hands he fought to free himself. For a second he thought he could breathe, but, as his vision began to blur, he knew he could no more breathe than he could escape.

He got a reverse grip on the knife, wrenched it from his belt and then stabbed backwards with the blade. Using all his strength he stabbed again, driving it time after time into the man behind him.

The wire slackened, allowing Redman to rip the noose away. He spun round, sweeping upwards with his knife hand.

There was no need. In front of him, Faisal Subhi stood transfixed. Blood from his abdomen was pouring down between his legs, dripping on to the floor.

The Arab staggered against a urinal. He spat at Redman, lifting the steel wire in one hand as if to come at him again.

Redman couldn't move, sickened by what he'd done and by the awful determination of the man.

Sinking to his knees, Subhi's expression changed. A moment later he was dead.

For Redman the nightmare wasn't over. He went to the wash-basin, unable to believe he had killed someone, understanding all too clearly now what Debbie had gone through on the peninsula.

He threw up twice, rinsing away the vomit while he let the water run over his hands. The panic caught him unawares – a sudden appreciation of where he was.

Unsteadily he walked to the door. It was locked from the inside. The Arab's precaution against being disturbed, Redman thought grimly. The only part of the plan that had worked.

After he'd dragged Subhi into a cubicle he sluiced some

water over the tiles then finished washing the blood off his hands. He was shaken badly, but with the body out of sight, his brain was beginning to function properly again.

He wondered if Subhi had been alone. Had Khatib landed more than one man in Darwin? Was there someone else inside the terminal?

At 9.30, as controlled as he was ever going to be, Redman went to find out. He headed straight for the exit, collar turned up to hide the weal around his neck, looking over his shoulder, walking casually in order not to draw attention to himself.

Not until he was outside the building did he start to feel less nervous. No matter how quickly the body was discovered, there was little or no chance of him being apprehended now. He was coming out of the shock, he thought. And in a few hours the Consortium were going to have a lot more trouble hunting him down.

Deciding it would be best to leave the airport until it was closer to the departure time of his flight to Port Moresby, he went back to the car, remembering on the way to wipe the knife before he dopped it into a culvert.

It was nearly ten when Redman drove out of the parking lot. Although there were fewer cars about than there had been earlier, making it easier to watch his mirror and look for other vehicles leaving the exit at the same time, he soon discovered his night vision was impaired, and that with each breath his eyes went out of focus.

Had he been more observant, or in less pain from his injured throat, he would have noticed a van pull out ahead of him. Instead, it wasn't until he'd overtaken it on the Pacific Highway that he became suspicious. It was a Bedford, the same model as the van that had been outside the apartment block last night. Redman could see its headlights in his mirror – two eyes following him wherever he went.

He pressed down on the accelerator, willing the little

Ford to go faster. Apart from an increase in the engine noise, nothing happened. The speedometer needle remained steady, hovering between fifty-five and sixty miles an hour depending on the gradient of the road.

To guard against a return of the panic, he told himself the van was a coincidence. Brisbane was full of Bedford vans. But if it wasn't a coincidence, if it was the same van, why hadn't Subhi acted last night when it would have been much safer? Why the hell wait until today? Unless it wasn't the COAS in the van at all.

Redman swore out loud. Until now the possibility hadn't occurred to him. But how could it be someone else? Or was it just conceivable that Corliss had somehow found out the truth?

The questions were coming too quickly. He had no answers, no explanations. And he was scared again. Had someone told Corliss? Trixie? Debbie? What had they said? Why had they? His head was swirling, a jumbled mess of uncertainty and doubt.

At Strathpine he turned off the highway, waiting to see if the van would follow. It did, closing on him before he could get the Ford up to speed again.

Because there was no chance of shaking off whoever was tailing him, Redman continued driving east towards the coast, looking for a shopping centre or some heavily populated area where he could lose himself. By now he was getting desperate, running out of adrenalin and running out of time.

He tried to follow street lights, picking roads he hoped would take him into Sandgate or Redcliff. But soon he was lost, travelling as fast as the Ford would go along a narrow unlit road beside a waterway.

Redman saw the lights of the van grow bigger in his mirror. They vanished suddenly as the driver pulled out to overtake.

The Bedford was alongside him now, beginning to edge forwards. When it swerved, Redman hit his brakes.

The van outbraked him easily, forcing him on to the shoulder at fifty miles an hour in a shower of gravel with his wheels locked. At the last moment Redman hauled the Ford back on to the road.

Ahead, the Bedford was slowing, weaving backward and forwards across the white line to prevent him from getting past.

A car had come up behind the Ford. The driver was flashing his lights to show his irritation. Boxed in, Redman did the only thing he could.

Yanking on the wheel, he put the Ford into a long sideways slide. As he did so, the car behind smashed into his rear fender as it went by, spinning him in a circle before it squeezed past the Bedford and disappeared.

Redman saw the van stop. At the same time, from the rear of it, came the flashes, sputtering bursts of gunfire.

His instincts betrayed him. Too frightened to move, he remained in the car. Only when the bullets tore open the door-panel did he throw himself out on to the road.

The waterway was close enough, a dark mirror at the bottom of an embankment twenty feet away. He was running hard when the first bullet hit him.

It didn't hurt at all. Nor did the next one.

Wondering why he'd stopped, he stood in the centre of the road, blinded by the headlights of an approaching car. It was the same car that had overtaken him, speeding back toward him, returning to see if he was all right.

Too late, Redman realized he had misunderstood.

He was dazzled, his head filled with the brilliance of a valley at the moment of ignition. Reaching into the valley with his hands, he felt the light wash over him. It was warm and inviting, and it was wonderfully soft.

Nine

She was a ballerina, pirouetting on tiptoe across the stage towards him. From where Redman stood, he could see beneath her skirt, see the swell of her calves and the curve of her thighs. She was so beautiful he ached to touch her.

On the far side of the stage a man appeared. He paused, then called out to Debbie. At once she ran to greet him, arms outstretched to show her pleasure.

Redman recognized the man, a solid, heavy man, ugly and unshaven, the cleaner from the IMT office with the tattooed hands. It was his hands she wanted. She took them in her own, stroking them, admiring them, running her fingers up his arm and making him draw his hands over her until the man responded. He held her by her pony-tail while he slowly peeled off her costume to expose the tattoos across her body.

Barely able to watch, Redman tried unsuccessfully to shout. His revulsion increased when he saw Debbie push her breasts against the cleaner's palms. She was laughing, exalted by her dancing, rejoicing in the union of his tattoos with hers.

The cleaner's hands were fluid, travelling over her skin, exploring every part of her with his fingertips.

This time when Redman yelled, she heard him. She turned and smiled, mocking him because he couldn't move. But he could. If he used all his strength, he could stop her. In front of him were the steps to the stage – all he had to do was climb them.

The pain went through him like a spear, driving him back into a pool of mist. Through it he heard Debbie's whispers. As usual she was taunting him, telling him how easily he had been deceived again.

Redman did what he'd done a dozen times before, using the mist to blank out the sound of her voice and the image of her bending over him.

Today it didn't work. She was still whispering, forcing him to hear her.

His rage mounted. For a moment the mist cleared, but it rolled back before he could see well enough to hit her. When it cleared again, someone else was bending over him – a girl Redman had never met before.

'Well, hello there.' She smiled. 'You're not going to go on making all that noise, are you?'

He stared at her. She was a nurse, dressed in a crisp white uniform.

'One question at a time,' she said. 'Otherwise we'll both get mixed up.'

He looked around him, trying to separate reality from unreality. 'Hospital,' he said.

'Not bad for a start, I suppose.' She shone a light in his eyes then put her hand round his wrist to take his pulse.

He tried to sit up in the bed but winced in pain. As well as having an immobilized left arm, he felt dizzy, and someone was hammering a nail into his chest.

'Does your head hurt?' she asked.

He nodded. 'A bit.'

'I'm Aliza Arens.' She released his wrist. 'I'm glad you've come round. You've been a lot of trouble to me. See if you can move the fingers of your left hand.'

'They're fine.' He didn't want to move his fingers.

'Where am I?'

'Ichilov Hospital. Just across from the art gallery and the museum.'

'I can go on being a lot of trouble,' Redman said.

She laughed. 'I'm sorry. I shouldn't be making fun of you. It isn't very professional, is it? You're in Tel Aviv.'

'Jesus Christ.'

'You've been here three days. The brigadier said you'd be surprised.'

Redman wasn't surprised. He was staggered.

'Long way from Australia,' she said. 'But you're American, aren't you?'

'Three days?' he said. 'Three days?'

'I'd better let someone know you're back with us.' She turned to go.

'Hang on. How did I get here?' What brigadier?'

'Ah.' She smiled again. 'I told you – one at a time. I think it'll be easier if someone else answers your questions. I'm only a nurse.'

He eased himself up on the pillows. This time it didn't hurt so much. 'You can tell me why I'm here, though,' he said. 'Can't you?'

'Well, because among other things you've been concussed, you have two bullet holes in your shoulder and because you were run over. Mind that drip.' She pointed at his arm. 'And stop trying to sit up. I'll go and telephone.'

Too bewildered to ask more questions, Redman watched her leave the ward. He struggled to think back, finding that the fantasy of Debbie was more vivid than his recollection of what had happened to him on the road from Strathpine. Although he could remember the waterway and the muzzle flashes spitting at him from the van, the memory of the car was indistinct. But that was three days ago, in another country, on the other side of the world. He was in Israel, in Tel Aviv, caught in a time-warp that defied the wildest logic he could think of.

Cautiously he moved his legs, then his arms and finally his fingers. With the exception of his strapped left arm everything worked. Only his chest was really painful, and provided he didn't move too quickly, that wasn't as bad as he'd first believed.

He probed around under the bandages, searching for something which might tell him how seriously he was injured. But it wasn't the injuries that mattered, he thought, it was the confusion; the impossibility of accepting that, by some means or other, a roadside in Brisbane had become a hospital ward in Tel Aviv.

More than anything Redman wanted to look out of the window. It was a necessity, a way to make certain this was not another dream.

With some difficulty he swung his legs on to the floor and tested them to see if they would bear his weight. He felt feeble, but the pain in his chest was a spur, helping him overcome the weakness.

Once on his feet he was able to carry the drip-stand over to the window with him. He used the stand to support himself, gripping it with his right hand while he leaned against the window-frame.

The view was disappointing, but different enough for him to know he was not in Australia. He'd never been anywhere like this, nor had he ever imagined being anywhere remotely like it. So if this was Tel Aviv, what the hell was he doing here?

The answers were starting to come when the nurse returned – an angry nurse. She escorted him firmly back to bed, beginning her lecture before she'd finished tucking in the sheets.

Redman stopped her. 'I know,' he said. 'And I won't do it again, I promise.'

She frowned at him. 'I don't believe you. Anymore than I believe those things you said while you were sedated. If you don't stay in bed, you won't heal up and I'll get into trouble.'

'What trouble's that?' The question came from a small, wiry man who came marching into the ward. He had extraordinarily dark eyes and a face of folded, worn-out leather.

'Steven.' He shook hands enthusiastically with Redman. 'Kershner. Yaron Kershner. Brigadier General, IDF. Glad you're awake. Are you as confused as I am?'

'I'm too confused to be confused,' Redman said.

'I'm sure you are. Still, better than being face down in a ditch somewhere in Queensland. Hell of a place for ditches. All those damn crocodiles, too.'

'You haven't come to talk about ditches,' Redman said. 'Have you?'

'No. I'm here to see how you're getting along and do the best I can to explain whatever you'd like me to explain.' Kershner's eyes twinkled. 'I imagine that's quite a lot.'

The nurse interrupted. 'Don't talk too long,' she said. 'Mr Redman has to rest.'

'I am resting,' Redman said. 'It's OK.'

'All right.' She glanced at Kershner. 'You're in charge. If he tries to get out of bed, push the buzzer. I'll give you half an hour.'

Kershner winked at Redman, waiting for her to leave before he made himself comfortable in a chair beside the bed. He produced some cigarettes, but thought better of it and put the packet away again.

'I suppose the first thing you want to know is what you're doing here?' he said.

'Tell me.'

'Debbie,' Kershner said. 'If it wasn't for her you wouldn't be anywhere.'

'You mean Melissa. Melissa Sarid.'

Kershner shrugged. 'I call her Debbie. She likes being called Debbie. It was her sister's name.'

'I know it was.'

'She telephoned from Brisbane,' Kershner said. 'I was

down in Sydney talking to the Australians about
supplying equipment for their new frigates. That was last
Wednesday night.'

'What's today?'

'May 25th. Tuesday. Why?'

Redman tried to work it out. 'That's six days ago,' he
said. 'The nurse told me I've been here three days.'

'I'll give you a run-down. Then you'll understand.
When Debbie called me, she was worried about a van that
had been parked outside your friend's apartment when
she left you. She had no idea whether the apartment was
being watched or not, but she was suspicious enough to
make the call.'

'Did she think it was Khatib?' Redman asked.

Kershner nodded. 'She couldn't be sure it was the
Consortium, of course. As things turned out, it wasn't,
but she didn't know then. Anyway, to cut a long story
short, she kept an eye on you until I arrived in Brisbane
early on Thursday. We followed you for most of the day
and wound up at the airport that night. The van had been
on your tail all afternoon so we knew something
interesting was going on.'

'But you didn't see Subhi?' Redman said.

'Not until I found him in the washroom.' Kershner
smiled. 'We foul up too from time to time. I don't know
how the Arabs located you. We were so hung up about
watching the van we never looked for another vehicle.'

'It was Corliss in the van,' Redman said. 'I'm sure it
was.'

'Probably US Security Council people. Debbie thinks
they bugged your friend's apartment. If she's right,
someone overheard the row you two had that night.'

'I was supposed to be working for Corliss,' Redman
said quietly. 'Did you know that?'

'Well, you sort of told Debbie, didn't you?' Kershner's
eyes were twinkling again. 'You must have been a big
disappointment to Corliss. One minute he believes he's

persuaded you to leak information to us – then the next minute he discovers you don't want anything to do with him or Project Omega. He must have wondered what the hell he'd done wrong.'

Redman looked at him. 'It was Debbie and I that went wrong,' he said.

'She told me.' Kershner was amused.

'Are you sure it was Americans who shot me? Just because I'd decided not to help Corliss?'

'Think about it. You were out of control. He couldn't afford to have you running around with the information he'd given you.'

'So I had the US and the Arabs on my back.' Redman paused. 'Has Debbie explained why the COAS wanted me out of the way?'

'She says it's because they found your friend's notes. They've realized their second airburst experiment isn't secret anymore.'

'It was the COAS who killed Owen,' Redman grunted. 'And the bastards tried to kill me. I told Debbie to be careful. She's in as much trouble as I am.'

'Not anymore she isn't.' Kershner took out his cigarettes again. 'Look, Steven, do you mind if I have one of these?'

'I don't. But Nurse Arens will. You're pushing your luck.'

Kershner went to open the window. He stayed there while he lit up. 'So there you are,' he said. 'Now you know.'

'No I don't. Was it you in the car?'

Kershner nodded. 'Sorry we didn't do a better job. We damn near killed you. Debbie ran you over. It was the only way we could get between you and the van.'

'What happened afterwards?'

'Who knows? The van took off right away.' Keshner blew smoke out of the window. 'Good thing it did, I suppose.'

'And you brought me here? To Israel.' Although the idea was still faintly unbelievable, Redman was beginning to understand.

'By military transport. Through Singapore and New Delhi. Debbie shot you full of morphine. We didn't have anything else. You can thank her for keeping you alive.'

'Where is she?'

Kershner looked at Redman briefly. 'In Tel Aviv. I called her before I came, but she said you wouldn't want to see her.'

'Because she knows you want my help. You want to know what Corliss told me, don't you?'

'Steven, that has to be your decision.' The brigadier was relaxed. 'We already have most of it. We know the Arabs were planning to carry out bomb tests in the Sinai Desert for our benefit. We know they've been playing around with explosive dust, and we understand there are certain limitations to what they can do with it.'

'The whole damn thing's a bluff.' Redman had made his decision. 'I don't care if that's classified information. Corliss can screw himself. The British have given the COAS all the technical data they need to produce enormous dust explosions and the Americans are trying to make you believe the Arabs have developed a superbomb.' He paused. 'I suppose that's treason.'

Kershner's face wrinkled. He was amused by Redman's expression. 'I don't think so,' he said. 'You see, while you've been catching up on your sleep, the US have had a major problem on their hands. Once they realized they'd blown it with you, they had to save face with Israel in a hurry. I hear the US Foreign Secretary damn near had a heart attack over it. That was before the Israeli Ambassador and three of our military advisors were called to the National Security Council to meet with some very anxious gentlemen from the Pentagon on Monday. They told us there aren't going to be any desert tests. As of two days ago, Project Omega is cancelled.'

Redman was astonished. 'Just like that,' he said. 'No Arab deterrent. The Consortium have just abandoned the whole thing?'

'Sure. It was a cheap enough project. What's the point of the Arabs conducting tests when we know what they're trying to do? The main problem now is foreign relations between Israel and the West. The US politicians are tearing their hair out – or they were until they came up with a nice explanation for their participation in Project Omega.'

'What explanation?' Redman said.

Kershner smiled. 'You'll like it,' he said. 'Officially, Britain and the US only ever agreed to be part of the project because they wanted to prevent the Arab states developing nuclear capability. The West was, in fact, helping Israel all along. They just forgot to tell us until now.'

'Christ,' Redman said. 'What do the Arabs think?'

'They think they've wasted a lot of time.' Kershner threw his cigarette-end out of the window. 'Not a happy ending for them.' He returned to the chair. 'Our problem is this peculiar second test in the Solomon Islands. The US doesn't know anything about it. Nor do we. I was hoping you'd be able to help us figure out whether we should still be worried.'

'Does Corliss know I'm here?' Redman asked.

'I told him. He doesn't like the idea much. He sounded upset when I spoke to him on the phone.'

'So everyone's friends again.' Redman said. 'Except for Jennifer and Warren Decker, and Owen. They died for nothing. And I wind up here in Tel Aviv with bullet holes in me.' He looked a Kershner. 'What happens to Corliss and Khatib?'

'Corliss might lose his job. That's about all. And Khatib will show up again somewhere else. You can bet on it. He has terrorist links with the Palestinians and with Libya. He's always going to be trouble. The Arabs knew all about

Khatib when they involved him with the testing program, but for some damn reason they decided he was the right man for the job at the time. They're probably hoping we'll find him.'

There was a cough from the door. Nurse Arens looked sternly at Kershner. 'Have you been smoking?' she asked.

'Not exactly.' Kershner smiled.

She came over to the bed. 'You've been talking for nearly an hour. That's enough for today. I'm afraid you'll have to leave now.'

'We're all done for the time being.' Kershner shook hands again with Redman. 'I'll come back in a few days,' he said. 'If you don't mind. You know why. Now, is there anything I can do for you? Phone your office in California or something?'

Redman shook his head. He felt dizzy again.

'OK.' Kershner turned round at the door. 'How about visitors?'

'No thanks.' Redman lay back on the bed to think. In his mind, more than anything it was the waste that hurt, the waste of lives to satisfy the political needs of the Middle East and to prop up the West's greed for Arab oil. Worse still, the project had even been a failure.

The nurse's voice intruded. 'Are you sure about visitors?' she said.

'Why?'

'Well, your friend's been every day. Each morning and every evening. Sometimes she was here for hours.'

'Debbie?' he said. 'Melissa Sarid?'

'She talked to you, I told her you couldn't hear, but she talked anyway. She gave me her phone number.'

'Call her now,' Redman said. 'I need to get this over with. Damn her.'

The nurse raised her eyebrows. 'I thought you – I mean —' Her voice faded. 'All right, then. As long as you promise to stay quiet.'

Over the next hour Redman fought the dizziness while

he endeavoured to come to terms with his feelings about Debbie. Mixed with them was an awareness that Kershner had been too careful – treading too warily whenever he'd mentioned Debbie. Because he was smart enough to understand a betrayal of trust was irreparable? Or did he simply believe it was none of his business?

But everything was Kershner's business, Redman thought. Just as it was obvious why the IDF had taken the trouble to bring him here. The IDF still wanted information – by whatever means they could get it.

For a while, despite his misgivings about confronting Debbie again, the aching for her returned. It was as if she were two people: the girl he thought had taken Josie's place and someone else altogether. But he could no more separate them than he could forget them. And he was tired – too tired to wonder what he would say to her if she came to see him.

He was asleep when the dream returned. In it, Debbie was bending over him, whispering his name again.

'Oh.' She drew back suddenly as he opened his eyes. 'I'm sorry.'

'It's OK.' Redman sat up.

'I wasn't sure you wanted to see me,' she said. 'That's why I haven't been before.'

The lie came so easily he could almost believe her. She was wearing a white cotton dress with a high collar, reminding him of how she'd always kept her blouse buttoned, how her clothes somehow always made her more desirable. Redman could see the outline of her breasts, the blemish near her lip and the golden flecks in her eyes. He hated her for being here.

'What's the matter?' She was concerned.

'You've been here every day. The nurse told me.'

She flushed. 'Because I was worried about you. First of all I ran you over in the car, and then I used too much morphine while we got you back to Brisbane and while we were waiting for the plane to come. If you'd died it would have been my fault.'

'Then I wouldn't have been able to tell Kershner anything, would I?'

Her cheeks went from red to white.

'I'm sorry,' he said. 'I didn't mean to say that. I wanted to thank you – for the rescue.'

'Do you think I did that for Kershner? Do you? Is that why you asked the nurse to phone me? So you could tell me to my face?'

'No.'

She managed to regain her composure. 'Did Kershner tell you Project Omega is over?'

He nodded. 'I guess we wasted our time.'

'No we didn't. We're the reason the Consortium's had to give up. We made them.'

'It was luck,' Redman said. 'We were lucky all along. If the COAS had found Owen's notes before Khatib found us on the peninsula we'd be dead too.'

'All because of the second test,' she said. 'It must have been terribly important to them.'

'Maybe it still is.' He met her eyes. 'Why else would I be talking to you in Tel Aviv?'

'This isn't going to work, is it?' She looked away. 'I shouldn't have come. You still think I don't care about us. You're not ever going to let me forget or get close to you again. Not now, not ever.'

'I didn't say that. You don't understand. Half the time I can't think of anything except us, then it all goes wrong inside my head because I don't know what you want from me. You're driving me crazy.'

'Well, that's a shame, isn't it?' She was tight-lipped. 'I don't want anything from you in the way you mean. I never have done.'

'It's Kershner who wants it – right?'

Turning her back on him, she walked to the door.

Through the dizziness he considered calling her back, but she was gone before he could think of what to say. But later, as he drifted off to sleep and the pool of mist rose up like a friend to meet him, he realized there had never been anything more to say.

In the four days between Kershner's first and second visits, Redman had grown weary of his own company. Even though he was on first-name terms with his nurse, and had spent countless hours talking with her on every subject either of them could think of, he was beginning to feel isolated from the real world and from the events which had brought him on the long journey to Israel. As a consequence, this morning, as well as enjoying being outside in the hospital grounds, his spirits had improved with the arrival of the brigadier.

'Would you rather sit in the shade?' Kershner asked.

'Hell no. This is great. I've missed the sunshine. You get used to it in Brisbane.'

'Are you going back to Australia?'

'I don't know yet. Haven't really thought much about it.' Redman stretched. 'It depends if it's safe, I suppose.'

'You're not a threat to anyone now. The whole thing's dead – except perhaps for understanding the reason for the second test. I'd like to get to the bottom of that if I can.' Kershner spread out a map on the grass. 'Show me where Decker's Eagle went down, would you?'

Redman found the Solomons. He pointed off the Malaitan coast. 'It's a guess. Based on an unconfirmed report from some fishermen who saw what they thought was lightning.'

'Look, Steven, are you sure an AT 302 couldn't fly that far out?'

'I'm sure. Their normal range is around three hundred and fifty miles. There are only two ways the Consortium could've set off an explosion in that part of the Pacific – either by fitting long-range fuel tanks to the dusters or by somehow refuelling them in flight. And both of those are lousy ideas. I don't know of any method of refuelling an

AT 302 in the air, and long-range tanks would take up cargo space. Tanks would reduce the amount of dust the planes could carry.'

Kershner frowned. 'Maybe they didn't need much dust, because of the extra oxygen from the magnesium perchlorate. Suppose the Arabs had an idea of developing a superbomb that only needed ten percent of the dust. That would make it a much more practical weapon.'

Redman nodded. 'Sure. I've already thought of that. But you still need a lot of dust – tons of it. That's the problem. Unless you have big military aircraft.' He glanced at Kershner. 'Do you know what the Japanese thought right after Hiroshima?'

'I can guess. It really is possible to make a dust explosion on that scale, is it?'

'I saw one,' Redman said. 'I don't know how it compares with a blast from a nuclear warhead but it's the scariest thing I've ever seen. Didn't Debbie tell you?'

Kershner lit a cigarette before he answered. 'She told me you probably saved her life.'

Redman smiled. 'That makes us even then. Except it's bullshit. We shouldn't even have been there. All I did was bury her in a foxhole. I damn near killed both of us.'

'Let me try this out on you. As far as we know – or you know – there was no sighting of the mother-ship off Malaita, only the squid boat. So, assume for a moment that the ship was somewhere else, out at sea. Now, imagine crop dusters loaded with enhanced dust being launched off the deck of it. Suppose the mother-ship was being used as a primitive aircraft carrier.'

Redman shook his head. 'I don't think it would work. Not unless the COAS were using some kind of launching catapult. Even if they were, there isn't enough deck space to land an AT 302, not even an empty one. There wasn't any evidence of a flight-deck on the ship we saw at Cape York.'

'OK.' Kershner's enthusiasm remained. 'So it has to be

in-flight refuelling.'

'How? From what? They only had two aircraft on Malaita.'

'The Consortium bought nine,' Kershner said. 'Remember? Through Patna Aviation in India. Perhaps the other seven were carrying fuel. They could've been flying from some other airstrip. There are airstrips everywhere in the Solomons.'

'I don't know.' Redman folded up the map. 'We might never know. You're trying too hard. I can't see it matters anyway. Even if the Arabs have the capability of attacking Israel with a bomb that only needs a small quantity of dust, one they could sneak through with one or two aircraft, why would they use it? The whole idea of Project Omega was to make you believe the Arab nations possessed a superbomb of some kind. But they never intended to use it. It was a deterrent – nothing else.'

Kershner stubbed out his cigarette. 'Sure,' he said. 'But if they have developed an enhanced bomb with fewer limitations, we need to know about it. You see, Steven, if the history of my country has taught us anything besides how to survive, it's that our future survival depends on us being ready to counter any threat of any kind from anywhere.' He smiled. 'Sorry. Sounds like an instruction from the IDF handbook, doesn't it? I expect you're right. We'll probably never know what our Arab friends were up to. It must be difficult for you to understand how we feel about these things.'

'No, I understand,' Redman said. 'I learned the hard way – from one of your experts.'

Kershner ignored the remark. 'How are all the aches and pains? You look pretty good to me.'

'I am. It's just the punctures in my shoulder.' Redman lifted his arm from the sling. 'This doesn't hurt anymore.'

'What about moving out of the hospital, then? If you like I can get you a flat near the beach at Givat Alijah. The IDF will be happy to pay, of course. It's the least we can do.'

'That'd be tremendous.' It was better than Redman had hoped for.

Kershner stood up. 'I'll arrange for someone to show you round Tel Aviv too. Don't want you wandering into some of the more exciting parts of town. Now, I'd be really grateful if you could do some more thinking about in-flight refuelling of AT 302s – just in case we're missing something obvious. Call me anytime you want to talk.'

Redman passed him the map. 'I need one more favour,' he said. 'There's a friend of mine in the Solomons, an islander called Jimmy Baura. He works at the Tambea Village Resort on Guadalcanal. Could you check he's OK for me and say I'll be telephoning him? After what happened to Owen I'd like to be sure everything's all right over there.'

'No messages for anyone else?' Kershner lit another cigarette.

'No,' Redman said. 'No one else at all.'

Ten

From the bedroom balcony Redman could just see the Mediterranean, no more than a glimpse of blue between the buildings, but a constant inducement for him to leave the flat so he could obtain a better view from somewhere else. As a result, each morning after breakfast for the last three days he'd set off into Givat Alijah, heading north on each occasion into Jaffa, losing himself in a maze of alleyways and courtyards until he reached the water. The ocean was a magnet, drawing him to it because the view from the balcony was so tantalizing, and because being by the sea somehow allowed him to think more clearly.

This morning, Redman wasn't thinking of anything. The technique worked better each time he tried it, a means of forgetting the mess that had finally ended with his discharge from Ichilov Hospital on Monday. Only if he thought of nothing for too long did the memories start to intrude, but he had learned how to handle them just as he had learned to ignore his dreams. Already they were occurring less frequently and soon, once he'd made the decision on what he was going to do with himself from here on, Redman was sure they would vanish altogether.

Leaving the balcony, he returned to the kitchen where

he dropped two more pieces of bread into the toaster. He was pouring a cup of coffee when the doorbell rang.

'Hang on,' he called. 'Won't be a minute.'

He put on a shirt and ran his fingers through his hair before going to find out what Kershner wanted today. So far, the brigadier had called at the flat four times, either to discuss some new theory or to drink beer in the evening while he talked about his job or the problems confronting Israel in a changing Middle East. Although Redman enjoyed his company, 9.30 in the morning was not the time for an encounter with Yaron Kershner.

It wasn't the brigadier. It was Debbie, standing awkwardly in the doorway waiting for Redman to ask her in.

'Hi,' he said. 'Coffee?'

'Please.' She followed him into the kitchen. 'Aren't you going to ask what I'm doing here?'

'What are you doing here?' Redman didn't know whether he was pleased to see her or not. On balance, he didn't think he was.

'Orders. I'm your tour guide.'

'Kershner's idea?'

'Do you mind?' She took the cup of coffee he offered her. 'I think he wants us to be friends.'

Redman smiled. 'We'd better try then, hadn't we?'

She relaxed slightly. 'How are you?'

'Fine. Give me a few more days and I'll be as good as new. Look.' He swung his arm.

'Oh.' She inspected the rope mark on his wrist then reached out to touch the weal around his neck. 'I thought about what you said when I saw you in hospital, you know, about us being lucky. I think we both were.'

Redman wished she'd keep her hands to herself. It was as if she was unconscious of what she was doing and the effect it had on him.

'The brigadier told me you've already been exploring,' she said. 'Do you want to go on by yourself?'

'Does that mean you'd rather I did?'

She looked at him over the rim of her cup. 'It means I'll understand if you'd prefer to have someone else show you around.'

'I can handle it if you can.'

'Are we friends?'

'Sure,' Redman said. 'Finish your coffee, then we'll go to the beach. There's supposed to be a great one south of here at a place called Bat Yam. A lady downstairs told me about it. We'll go swimming.'

'It's a bit difficult for me.' She faltered. 'You know – because – swimming. I'll have to wear a shirt or something.'

He cursed himself for being so stupid. 'Dolphinarium,' he said. 'Then the Great Mosque and the Shalom Tower. Anywhere.'

'Why don't you leave it to me? I live here, remember?'

'I'll buy you lunch if you teach me Hebrew – so I can read the street signs.' He held the door open for her. 'Come on. Let's go.'

Despite her smile as she slipped past him, he was certain she was no happier with Kershner's arrangement than he was. But she was only doing what she'd been told to do, Redman thought. And the smile came with the job.

He followed her downstairs, wondering whether he was making a mistake, and how long it would be before he was used to being with her again. But outside in the sunshine, mingling with a thousand other people on the street, he found that being with her was easier than being without her. Confused by his feelings, he set off with his guide, unaware that this morning was the beginning of what would turn out to be not a single day of confusion, but countless, sun-filled summer days which blended one into another as he struggled to rationalize his thoughts.

For nearly three weeks, from the Quasila Tell hill in the north of the city to the old settlement of Migdal Afeq in the east and the palm-fringed Russian Monastery in Jaffa, he explored Tel Aviv more thoroughly than the most dedicated tourist. There were evenings in restaurants, mornings spent wandering along the beach and there were sunsets from the balcony that flooded the flat with yellow light as though the whole of the city was aglow.

And through it all, for every moment he was with her, running like a thread through everything he did, everywhere he went, was the awareness of the girl beside him. It was another dream: one in which she was again two people – the girl he wanted her to be and his tour guide from the IDF, supplied by Kershner to repay some imagined debt.

Early in the morning while it was still cool, she was the guide. But in the evening when she sat on the balcony rail, humming softly to herself, looking out between the buildings to the pale-blue strip of the ocean, it was the girl he'd taken to the peninsula who occupied his mind.

Night after night he remembered her, knowing that by choosing to remember he was making things worse. His distraction continued to build until, on one warm Wednesday morning, Redman made the decision to confront the problem once and for all.

They were in Jaffa, resting in the shade of a 16th century wall by the Franciscan church of St Peter, when he told her they had to talk.

'Now?' she said. 'Here?'

'We'll go back to the flat. We can go to it through there.'

'All right.' She sounded doubtful. 'Are you sure this is a good idea?'

'No. But we can't go on like this.'

She didn't answer, walking in silence while he led her back through the artists' quarters and took the short cut across to Yefet Street. Redman, too, was quiet, uncertain yet of what he should say and worried she might reject his suggestion.

His timing was bad. Parked at the kerb outside the flat was a black Peugeot. It displayed a small flag bearing the insignia of the IDF.

The driver came to meet them, speaking to Debbie in Hebrew while he held the car door open for her.

'We have to leave,' she said. 'Both of us. Some kind of emergency.'

'Like what?' Redman asked.

'I don't know. The driver has instructions to take us to the Hayarkon Building the minute we got back. Kershner's been waiting since ten o'clock.'

'So much for you and me.'

She smiled. 'There'll be another time. This sounds fairly urgent.'

The urgency became more apparent when the Peugeot entered the traffic. After using his telephone, the driver put his foot down, forcing his way across town, not once reducing speed until the car drew up outside the headquarters of the IDF.

A soldier met them on the sidewalk, a young Israeli girl dressed in uniform and armed. She escorted them inside, accompanying them in the elevator to the third floor before showing them to an anteroom in the west wing of the building. Kershner was waiting in the doorway.

'Sorry about the rush,' he said. 'I only heard a few hours ago.'

'Heard what?' Redman asked. 'What's going on?'

'We have a problem. Washington called last night to say some friends of yours were coming.' He put up his hand to stop any further questions. 'I'll explain in a minute.'

Redman followed Kershner and Debbie into a smoke-filled board room. At one end, seated at a table were two men – a US colonel and a British commander. Neither man made any attempt to rise.

Kershner approached the table, speaking first to Corliss and Slater. 'I think we all know each other,' he said, 'so I won't bother with introductions.' He turned to Debbie. 'Make yourself comfortable – you too, Steven. This might take a while.'

Redman sat down, trying to refocus his thoughts, dragging his mind back to another meeting, one for which he had been equally unprepared.

'Right,' Kershner said. 'At the risk of wasting time, I'll give you an outline of what's happened. Colonel Corliss and Commander Slater can correct me if I have anything wrong.'

Corliss was annoyed. 'Do we have to do this in front of Redman and Miss Sarid?' he said.

'We do it however I want to do it.' Kershner's voice was clipped. 'I'll begin with the aircraft.' He glanced at Redman. 'Steven, you remember our conversation about the Consortium buying nine AT 302s through Patna Aviation?'

Redman nodded. 'Is this about flight refuelling?'

'I wish it was. No, this is about the seven spare aircraft that weren't used for the airburst and groundburst experiments in the southern hemisphere – seven AT 302s that the COAS reserved for the exhibition tests in the Sinai Desert. Two days ago, the Pentagon received a joint communique from Damascus, Cairo and Amman about them. The planes were in storage in Alexandria. But now they're not. They've disappeared. As soon as the Consortium found the planes were missing they contacted Washington. Washington has alerted us.'

Despite the implications, Redman couldn't believe they were serious enough to have brought Corliss and Slater to Israel.

'Interesting, don't you think, Steven?' Kershner lit a cigarette. 'Particularly because it's not only the dusters that are gone. Nassim Khatib has disappeared as well.'

'When?'

'A few days after the Consortium radioed his mothership to say Project Omega was cancelled. Khatib was instructed to sail for the Gulf of Aden and come up through Suez into the Mediterranean. Since then the COAS haven't been able to contact either him or the ships.'

'Look, Kershner,' Corliss interrupted, 'you're making it sound as though the US hasn't done anything for three weeks. You and your government should understand we didn't know about Khatib until the Arabs told us the planes were missing. If they'd got in touch earlier about the ships we might have been able to track them by satellite but it's a bit damn late now. We're trying like hell but we've only had two days to do it in.'

Kershner smiled. 'Not your fault, Colonel. Anymore than the British could've anticipated something like this happening to the planes they bought for the COAS. It's ironic, though, isn't it? Here's a threat to Israel's national security and it's the Arabs who have let us know.'

'Hang on,' Redman said. 'Are you trying to say Khatib intends going ahead with a desert test by himself? Why would he? There's no point. Israel knows a dust bomb is damn near impossible to use tactically. The Consortium will have told Khatib the party's over. He knows Israel isn't going to be fooled by some bloody great explosion in the desert.'

'The Arabs aren't worried about a desert test,' Kershner said. 'Nor are we. If Khatib's gone off the rails and wants to explode a dust bomb over the Sinai, we don't care. It's worse than that – or it may be.'

'You're damn right it is,' Corliss said. 'I'll tell you what the Arabs are worried about, what the US is worried about too. Now we've heard the background to this second Solomon Island experiment we're certain Khatib's had his own agenda for a while. He's had his own private development programme running for months, just in case something went wrong with Project Omega. We think he's produced a second generation bomb, one that needs far less dust; maybe one he can deliver to a target with just a few planes. Now, if we're right, why would he bother with a demonstration? Why not use it to do some real damage?'

'He'd be crazy.' Before Redman finished speaking he realized his mistake.

Kershner saw his expression. 'Neat, isn't it,' he said. 'Khatib knows Israel won't retaliate. We can't launch a retaliatory attack on Cairo or Damascus or Amman or anywhere, because it's the Arabs who have given us the warning. By tomorrow half the newspapers in the world will have the story – the Arabs will make sure they do. Some mad Syrian terrorist might be planning something unpleasant for Israel, but we can hardly blame our neighbours, can we? Not when they've apologized for Project Omega and not after it was them who sounded the alarm about Khatib to start with.'

Debbie spoke for the first time. 'Suppose the Consortium had this idea all along,' she said. 'Let Israel find out about Project Omega, say they're sorry, then pretend they're concerned at what Khatib might do. It's a perfect double-cross.' She paused. 'And we can't do anything about it.'

'We have to,' Kershner said. 'Why do you think the colonel and the commander are in Tel Aviv? We have the full military support from the US and from Britain if we need it. And the Arabs have said they'll report on anything that might help us along.'

'The Arabs don't have to help,' Redman said. 'Why should they? All they have to do is make the right noises.'

'You're politically naïve, Redman,' Corliss said. 'And cynical. Israel can count on Arab assistance. The US has made that clear. There's diplomatic pressure being put on the Consortium from Washington. The Arabs can't afford a major incident at the moment. The last thing they want is the destruction of an Israeli city. It'd set back negotiations on the Palestinian question for a decade.'

'Khatib wouldn't bomb a city,' Debbie said.

Kershner was less confident. 'Depends what he has in mind,' he said. 'We don't know what he can do with an enhanced dust bomb.' He directed his attention to Slater. 'Which is what the commander is going to tell us, I hope.'

Slater had been listening impassively, waiting for an opportunity to speak.

'Indeed,' he said. 'Perhaps the first thing I should do is warn you about the peculiarities of large dust explosions. You see, Brigadier, you may believe all you have to do is detect Khatib's AT 302s by radar and simply shoot the planes down. I'm afraid it's more complicated because destroying the aircraft doesn't destroy the dust. High-technology weapon systems such as air-to-air or ground-to-air missiles are designed to neutralize high-technology warheads. Here you're dealing with something quite different. Shooting down the crop dusters will just disperse their pay-loads into the atmosphere.'

'That's not a hell of a lot of dust though,' Redman said. 'Not compared with what we saw in Australia. On the peninsula, the Consortium had AT 302s flying for nearly two hours and even then they probably only spread a small proportion of the dust in the valley. Most of it came from the pylon. Khatib only has seven aircraft and the most they could carry is about a ton each.'

Slater peered over his glasses. 'But that wasn't enhanced dust, was it, Redman? You don't seem to be thinking clearly. We don't know how powerful seven tons of enhanced dust might be. Only Khatib knows that.'

Kershner lit another cigarette. 'So how do we handle a cloud of enhanced dust?' he said.

'You're dealing with atomized aluminium and aluminium flakes,' Slater said. 'Plus extremely fine coal dust with the probable addition of something like twenty percent magnesium perchlorate. That's a dangerously unstable mixture. It has a wide ignition window.'

'What does that mean?' Kershner said.

'Well, when a dust mixture is scattered into the atmosphere, to begin with the concentration in a given volume of air is very high. As the dust disperses, the concentration reduces. Eventually the dust will thin out until the concentration is too low for it to explode. But between the time of high concentration and the time of low concentration there's a period when the dust will be combined with just the right amount of air or oxygen. During that period it'll detonate with extreme violence. We call the period an ignition window.'

Kershner frowned. 'So once we have a dust cloud, sooner or later it'll reach an explosive concentration no matter what we do.'

Slater nodded. 'Somewhere in the cloud the conditions will be ideal for detonation. But you still have to trigger the blast, of course. The Consortium used dynamite triggers.'

'You can stop it,' Redman interrupted. 'With inerting powder or water.'

Slater raised his eyebrows. 'Have you suddenly become an expert?'

'Not me. A friend of mine was. But he's dead – like a lot of other people. And you don't give a damn, do you, Slater? This is just a nice academic exercise for you.'

Slater continued as though he hadn't heard. 'Moisture or rain in the atmosphere will inhibit the ability of the dust to detonate,' he said. 'So will the addition of an inert, non-combustible dust or powder like chalk. I suppose you could employ military aircraft to disperse clouds of chalk on to any dust layers released by Khatib's AT 302s. Of course there's no guarantee the chalk would mix quickly enough with the aluminium and the coal, but it might be worth a try. The only other solution is to eliminate any source of ignition. That's probably impossible if you shoot down the aircraft because of flames, sparks and high-temperature wreckage.'

Kershner slumped into a chair. 'I don't believe it,' he said. 'Here we are, one of the best-armed countries in the world with billions of dollars worth of high-technology defence, and all we can do is hope it rains on the day Khatib decides to make his move.'

'You'll have to get to him first,' Corliss said. 'Or knock the dusters out of the sky the minute they're airborne.'

'Sure.' Kershner was thinking. 'If we can find him.

What chance is there of your people picking up the ships by satellite reconnaissance?'

'Pretty good. We're working on it.'

Redman shook his head. 'Khatib won't be on the ship. He's here in the Middle East somewhere. How else could seven AT 302s vanish into thin air?'

Leaving his chair, Kershner went over to pull down a map of the Middle East. 'Could you transport them by road?' he asked.

'Yes,' Redman said. 'They're not all that big. Don't forget Khatib had two on board the mother-ship. If you take the wings off an AT 302 you can move it in a truck.'

'So where's he going to come from?' Kershner used a wooden pointer to trace flight paths on the map. 'From here, over the Sinai from Egypt? Down from Syria, or across from Jordan?'

'God knows.' Redman studied the map. 'Depends on his range.'

'Which brings us back to flight refuelling,' Kershner said. 'And what his target is.'

'Target,' Redman said suddenly. 'Christ.' He turned to Debbie. 'The airline brochures from IMT – do you still have them?'

Her eyes widened. 'They're upstairs in an office – with the photos from Cape York.'

'What are you talking about?' Kershner left the map, colliding with Debbie who was already on her feet.

'Excuse me,' she said. 'I won't be a minute. It's a long shot.'

As soon as she left the room, Redman walked over to Corliss. 'In case I don't get another chance you'd better hear this while Debbie's out of the way,' he said. 'And if you try to get out of that chair, I'll kick you in the balls so hard you'll never be any good again. Now you listen to me, you son of a bitch. When this is over, however it turns out, I'm coming after you. I'm going to crucify you, Corliss. If you thought Oliver North had a problem, you're wrong. By the time the newspapers and Congress are through with you, your wife won't even say hello. You'll be lucky if you stay out of jail.'

Corliss began to stand up but found himself thrust back into his chair the instant he moved. His cigarette and a sheaf of papers dropped to the floor.

Redman picked them up, throwing the papers at him before Kershner could intervene.

'Steven, give me the cigarette,' Kershner said. 'You've made your point. Now leave it alone. We have more important things to do.'

Redman stubbed out the cigarette in an ashtray. He was pleased to see Corliss had gone white.

Kershner was less pleased. Whatever he thought of Redman's outburst, he was careful to show his disapproval, helping Corliss gather up the papers while he apologized. Only Slater was amused, leaning back in his chair with a slight smile on his lips.

'How long's Debbie going to be?' Kershner said. 'We need to get on with this.'

'I'm here.' She re-entered the board room, carrying the brochures under her arm.

'Have you looked?' Redman asked.

'Not yet.' She gave him some. 'I've been thinking, though. It won't be any good. These only show flight routes over the South Pacific – mostly anyway.'

'It doesn't matter,' Redman said. 'We're not interested in flight routes – not this time. All we need is a world map with the Middle East on it. Any damn map.'

Debbie found one in the French UTA brochure. She inspected it closely but shook her head.

Redman was equally unlucky, discovering most of the brochures either had no maps of the right area or that they were too small to be of any practical use. Only one showed promise, a glossy Lufthansa publication having a large-scale, fold-out map attached to the rear cover. It showed the western coast of the Mediterranean, the Red

Sea and part of the Indian Ocean.

Holding the page up to the light, Redman saw the pinhole at once – a tiny dot glowing like a beacon in Israel's Negev Desert.

'It's all right,' he said quietly. 'It's not a city.'

Debbie moved across to see. 'Oh my God,' she breathed.

Quickly she took the brochure to the wall map, checking the position of the pinhole before she turned round.

'Dimona,' she said. 'Khatib's going to bomb Dimona.'

There was silence in the room. Corliss appeared to be particularly shocked, sitting motionless with his hands on the table in front of him.

Redman was the first to speak. 'We should have guessed,' he said.

'Why.' Kershner's face was grim. 'How the hell could we have guessed?'

'Don't you see? It's a reverse deterrent. Omega was supposed to stabilize the Middle East by making Israel believe the Arabs had a weapon that was as powerful as a nuclear bomb. But there's another way to create a balance of power – by wiping out Israel's Nuclear Centre at Dimona – by making sure Israel can't ever produce nuclear weapons again. It'll work just as well.'

Kershner started pacing round the room. 'And we can't retaliate,' he said. 'God in heaven.'

'It could be worse,' Slater said. 'Your nuclear warheads aren't stored at Dimona. Attacking the reactor might damage your ability to produce more plutonium 239, but you'll still have a stockpile of nuclear weapons, won't you?'

'So what,' Kershner retorted. 'We can't use them. And Khatib knows we can't.'

Debbie studied the brochure again. 'There's no circle,' she said. 'And no date either. We don't know when.'

Kershner stopped pacing. 'But we do know Khatib

won't get through,' he said. 'Not with AT 302s. It'll be like shooting sparrows. But if that won't stop the dust exploding, we'll have to evacuate half the villages and settlements in the Negev.' He glanced at Corliss. 'I expect twenty-four-hour satellite surveillance and early warning coverage of all our borders by United States airborne radar. On top of that I shall require US transport aircraft capable of dispersing water and inert dust at high altitude and the guaranteed cooperation of the Syrian, Jordanian and Egyptian Governments. Is that clear?'

Corliss nodded. 'I'll call Washington this afternoon.'

'Now,' Kershner said. 'You'll do it now. We may not have until this afternoon.'

Eleven

The rail around the catwalk was too hot to touch, and beneath his feet the steel grating was no cooler. Redman could feel the heat seeping through the soles of his shoes. It made him wonder what conditions were like for the people in the convoys.

He could see a convoy in the distance now, a caterpillar of trucks coming from Yerokam, grinding its way north through the desert towards Beersheba or Jerusalem where its passengers of men, women, children, sheep and goats would be unloaded before the trucks returned to evacuate some other village.

The whole of the central Negev was on the move, he thought. Settlers, Bedouins, tourists and even non-essential personnel from the military bases were on the roads, travelling in temperatures of over a hundred degrees through a parched landscape of sand and mountains to what was supposed to be a safer place.

For five days the convoys had been working in the zone, leaving one after another, day and night, until Redman had lost count of how many of them there had been. And ever since they'd begun, he'd been worrying about the operation – a huge undertaking based on nothing more definite than a pinhole in an airline brochure.

He turned his eyes away, looking out instead over the palm trees which surrounded the Dimona compound.

The reactor was ugly, a squat ribbed dome shining in the sunlight, reminding him of Three Mile Island and of pictures he'd seen of other nuclear installations. They were all ugly, he thought. But somehow, because this one was in the middle of the desert, it seemed particularly forbidding.

From his vantage point on the catwalk he could see most of the other surface buildings too, windowless, single-storey blocks concealing the eight underground levels where the real work of the Dimona Centre was carried out. The palm trees were incongruous, Redman decided, a freakish addition to a place where trees had no business being, any more than fresh green grass should be growing on top of subterranean machons producing weapon-grade plutonium.

'Well?' Kershner had come to join him on the catwalk. 'Are you satisfied?'

'I don't know. How thick's the concrete on the machons?'

'Seven or eight feet. It's not just to protect the processing chambers from air attack, it's a radiation shield for the workers, too. We put nearly a hundred tons of spent-fuel elements through here every year.'

Redman pointed to a reinforced water tank. 'What's that for?'

'Cooling. The reactor elements spend fourteen weeks in there to get rid of the worst of the volatile iodine – 131. We can't handle the elements properly without cooling them off first, not even with remote handling equipment. Radioactive iodine – 131 – is nasty stuff.'

'It's just the reactor and the cooling tank then,' Redman said. 'If everything else is underground I can't see there's much of a problem. Anyway, Khatib's not going to get within ten miles of here, is he? You're worrying about nothing.'

Kershner smiled. 'I'd be more worried if he was using missiles or high-performance combat aircraft.'

'They wouldn't get through, either,' Redman said. 'You've got Patriots, Chapperelle and Hawk anti-missile-missiles everywhere. This must be the most heavily guarded place on earth.'

'Missiles rely on infra-red or radar guidance systems. Suppose we can't pick up the AT 302s on our radar for some reason. Suppose the planes start releasing aluminium flakes before we get a fix on them. That'll blind the radar. All we'll see is one big blur on our screens.'

'You still have infra-red,' Redman said. 'Your missiles will home-in on the heat from the dusters' engines.'

'Perhaps.' Kershner smiled again. 'So you think our Nuclear Centre's safe, do you?'

'Sure. It's the villages that are vulnerable. If Slater's right, once the AT 302s are in the air there's nothing you can do except make sure the explosion happens where you want it to happen. That's fine so long as Dimona's the target. If it isn't, you'll have to kill the dusters somewhere else – in the most underpopulated area you can find. It's not whether you can shoot the planes down, it's where. I never realized so many people lived in the Negev.'

'We can't evacuate them all,' Kershner said. 'But I figure we'll have cleared out everyone over a twenty-five-mile radius from here by tomorrow night. That gives us a pretty good buffer zone.'

'In the end it comes back to the quantity of dust.' Redman paused. 'But Khatib can't do too much damage with seven tons of it whether it's enhanced or not.'

'Still be better to hit him on the ground, though,' Kershner said. 'If we knew where the hell he was.' He glanced at Redman. 'Which brings me to a question I have for you, Steven.'

'I don't have any more answers. I'm all thought out.'

'It's not about the attack. It's about Khatib. You see, one way or the other, either before or after his planes are airborne, I have to find him.'

'To stop him from trying a second time?' The thought had crossed Redman's mind earlier.

'Israel can't afford to go through this again. I need to be sure he hasn't got another batch of AT 302s hidden away somewhere.'

'So what's the question?' Redman asked.

'Well, to be honest, I don't believe we'll have any luck finding Khatib until he makes his move. But the minute he does, we'll have a fix on the take-off point of the AT 302s – an airstrip, a road or something. And that's where Khatib will be.' Kershner stopped to light a cigarette before he went on. 'You see, Steven, I've been authorized to command a small rapid-response unit which has just one main objective. I'd like you to be part of that unit.'

'To capture Khatib?'

'If we can. You and Debbie know what he looks like. All the IDF has are some photos of him. The plan is for the Sayerat Golani to go in by helicopter, destroy his ground equipment, and bring Khatib back to Israel for questioning.'

'You're going to cross borders?' Redman said. 'Fly into Syria or Egypt if you have to?'

'There isn't any other way. The US is prepared to tell the Arabs what we're doing if they have to, but Corliss won't alert anyone unless something goes wrong.' Kershner hesitated. 'Of course we don't know what we could run into. How are you with a gun?'

'I'll take a semi-automatic rifle,' Redman said. 'Something that shoots flat. I don't want anything fancy.'

Kershner raised his eyebrows. 'You can have a heavy machine-gun if you want one.'

Below the catwalk at ground level, the palm trees were rustling. A moment later Redman felt the breeze, hot air coming down through the Jordan valley from the north. It grew stronger, driving flurries of sand across the compound. He felt the sweat dry on his skin, and became aware of an immediate drop in humidity.

'You can tell the convoys to slow down.' Redman pointed to Kershner's cigarette smoke. 'There's too much wind for dust today.'

'It'll ease when the sun goes down,' Kershner replied. 'But not much at this time of year. If it carries on, we'll be in for a wait.'

Redman remembered waiting on the promontory, searching for clouds, watching tufts of grass to gauge the strength of the wind. It seemed a long time ago now.

'No chance of rain, I suppose,' he said.

'Once in two hundred years.' Kershner grinned. 'But somehow I don't think we'll be that lucky.' He started off back along the catwalk. 'You don't want to spend any more time up here, do you?'

'No. Thanks for the tour, though. I've never been this close to a nuclear reactor before.'

'Your other tour guide said I shouldn't ask you to come with us.' Kershner continued walking. 'She thinks you're about ready to head back to the States or to wherever it is you're going.'

'I am ready,' Redman said. 'But I'm not going anywhere until this is finished.'

The range officer inspected Redman's target through his spotting scope. 'Where did you learn?' he asked.

Redman lowered his rifle. It was a .308 calibre SIG which seemed to shoot better each time he used it.

'Long story,' he said.

'I'm not going anywhere.' The officer sat down. 'We train some pretty good marksmen here, but our guys don't practise much at the distances you shoot over.'

'My father was a bow-hunter,' Redman said. 'I grew up with bows – got my first deer with one when I was thirteen. After hauling on a hunting bow, the minute I picked up a rifle it seemed so easy I thought I was cheating. That was when I was about sixteen. Since then, I've spent a lot of time with a rifle in open country – you know, shooting at woodchucks, rabbits and things.'

The officer brushed the sand off his overalls. 'Maybe the IDF should train with bows.' He smiled. 'The day's warming up. You'd better get inside before you melt.'

When the officer had gone, Redman unloaded the SIG and removed the magazine, surprised to find how warm the sun had made the gun. It wasn't until he was walking back to the barracks that he realized why the afternoon had suddenly become so hot.

Every day since the 29th of June, the desert wind had made conditions tolerable if not exactly pleasant. And each day for the last six, like everyone else at the Ramon airbase, Redman had waited for the wind to drop while he prepared for an alert that hadn't come. He had practised on the outdoor range, attended planning meetings and studied maps until he had almost convinced himself the wind would blow from the north forever.

But as quickly as it had begun nearly a week ago when he'd been standing on the catwalk at Dimona, now it had stopped. In its place was a westerly breeze – one that was nearly as hot, but one that Redman guessed was gentle enough to give Khatib an opportunity to launch the AT 302s if he was ready to attack.

Redman's fears were soon confirmed. Shortly before 2.30 in the afternoon the airbase siren began to wail. He'd heard it before – each morning at 6.30 – a short burst of noise to test the system. But this was different, a continuous, high-pitched scream making him hurry to the briefing room where the sixteen members of Kershner's team were already starting to assemble.

Among them was Debbie. Although this was the first he'd seen of her since the meeting with Corliss and Slater in Tel Aviv, when she came across to sit beside him, Redman found himself at a loss for words.

'Welcome to the Sayerat Golani,' she whispered. 'You're mad letting Kershner talk you into this.'

'No one talked me into it.'

'Shh. Here he is.'

The brigadier strode into the room, going straight over to the illuminated map. 'Tell someone to stop that damn siren,' he said. It went off as he finished speaking.

'Right.' Kershner turned to face his audience. 'This isn't a scramble. If it was, we'd be out of here in a couple of minutes. This is something else. We've just heard one of the US keyhole photo reconnaissance satellites has located the squid boat in the Red Sea. It's anchored in the mouth of the Gulf of Aqaba. According to the Pentagon there's an eighty-seven percent outline correlation with the photographs taken at Cape York, so we're as sure of it as we can be.'

'No mother-ship?' Redman asked.

'Not yet. We already have a frigate and two surveillance aircraft in the area but they've found nothing else so far. The squid boat's probably not a problem, though. We're more interested in this.'

Using a flow pen, Kershner drew a red rectangle on the map. 'You'd better gather round and take a look.'

The rectangle was in Jordan. Redman estimated it to be ten or twelve miles over the Israeli border, half-way along a dotted line joining the Jordanian villages of Qasr et Tilha and Rashadiya.

'We have French and US satellite evidence of troop movements here on this dirt road.' Kershner pointed to the line. 'As you can see, it's the middle of nowhere, south-east of us and around forty-seven to fifty miles from Dimona. That makes it an ideal place for Khatib to mount an operation.

'We've asked the Jordanians if they have trucks or men in the area. Until we hear back from them we can't do anything except get ready. Jordan has confirmed the road could be used as an airstrip for AT 302s but they refuse to let us do a fly-over to take a look.

'In the meantime, while we're covering the border with ground and airborne radar, the US has two C5A Galaxies on the runway at Uvda in case we need the chalk. They won't take off unless we have solid target information. Until we do, I want the helicopter crew and the combat team on a one-minute standby.'

'Sir, what about the squid boat?' Someone behind Redman asked the question.

Kershner glanced at his watch. 'We've decided not to take any chances. There's an F16 in the air right now. Engagement will be in just under three minutes.'

From 22,000 feet, the Gulf of Aqaba was a fifteen-mile wide finger of blue water pointing at the bottom tip of the Negev. To the west, the brown-stained southern mountains of the Sinai stretched away into the haze and, to the east, for as far as the pilot of the F16 could see, the Saudi desert was laid out like a faded, yellow carpet.

Taking care not to violate Saudi airspace, he banked the aircraft, reducing altitude before commencing his first run towards the tiny islands guarding the mouth of the Gulf.

Below him, surface detail became more distinct. He could pick out groups of fishing boats and see freighters heading north into the more heavily trafficked Gulf of Suez.

After radioing both pilots of the surveillance planes he made contact with the frigate, repeating his target coordinates and asking for confirmation. He felt calm and dispassionate, as though this was a practice run or an exercise in the simulator. Not until he saw the squid boat did his pulse begin to quicken.

The *Zhongshan* had fared badly on its voyage from the Solomon Islands and Cape York. Most of the hull was streaked in rust and paint was flaking from the superstructure below the bridge. Only on the stern was there a fresh, white daub of paint where a further attempt had been made to obliterate its name while the squid boat had lain in hiding at Bur Safaga off the Egyptian coast. The paint made it easier, a white centre on an otherwise drab and dirty target.

At anchor, floating quietly in the sunlight on an almost completely tranquil sea, the *Zhongshan* swam into the sights of the F16.

The pilot saw his bracketing lights flicker. At once he pressed the button on his stick.

Raked with cannon-fire from bow to stern, the squid boat shuddered as the F16 roared skywards to prepare for its second run.

No crew appeared on the deck of the *Zhongshan* – no lifeboats were launched and the flag at the head of its one remaining mast continued to flutter in the breeze. It fluttered for another twenty seconds. Then, as salvo after salvo of rockets tore into the rusted fabric of its hull, the *Zhongshan* died.

For a while, flames from burning wreckage and leaking fuel burned upon the surface of the Gulf, but soon there was only an oil slick to mark the place where the squid boat finally lay at rest upon the ocean floor.

It was dark when the siren at the airbase wailed again. This time, although Redman ran for the briefing room, he was too late to hear Kershner's opening remarks.

The brigadier was drawing a line on the map, a straight red line joining Dimona to the rectangle inside the Jordanian border.

'We have seven angels,' Kershner said. 'Closing at a little under a hundred-and-eighteen miles an hour. That gives them a flight time of twenty-four minutes to the target centre. Ground and air defence will wait until the planes are well inside our evacuated zone before they knock them out which means that between twelve and fifteen minutes from now there's going to be one hell of a big bang in the eastern sector.

'By then we have to be clear of the sector and on our way to the Jordanian border. According to airborne radar we'll have a minimum of thirteen vehicles to deal with when we get to where we're going, maybe more. We won't know how many for sure until we're on the ground. Anyone got any questions before we move out?'

There was a shuffling of feet and some discreet coughing but no questions.

'OK.' Kershner switched off the lights behind the map. 'Let's do it.'

Outside, the twin rotors of a Sea Knight were blowing sand across the tarmac into Redman's face. Crouching low, he ran for the forward hatch with his eyes half shut, waiting until he was inside before he opened them fully to check for Debbie.

She was seated next to Kershner in the rear of the helicopter, distinguishable only by the pony-tail protruding from her helmet. Redman returned her wave.

A sergeant beside him shouted over the whine of the turbines. 'Do you know her?'

'Sort of' Redman yelled. 'Why?'

The sergeant grinned. 'Every other bastard in here thinks she was waving at them.'

The whine of the gas turbines increased and the Sea Knight began to tip as its front wheels left the ground. A second later the helicopter was airborne, rotors chopping hard to gain altitude and forward speed. It swung east over the unlit airbase, travelling more quickly while the pilot set his course and transmitted his flight route to the ground control officer at Dimona.

'Better get ready.' The sergeant unbuckled his harness. 'You never know.'

He stepped over Redman's feet and began feeding a cartridge belt into the floor-mounted machine-gun beside the hatch. On the opposite side of the fuselage, another machine-gun was being loaded. Redman watched the preparations, trying to decide whether he was scared or excited and wondering what an explosion of seven tons of dust might look like in the dark. In his head he started to calculate how far away the Sea Knight would be at the instant of ignition.

The calculation occupied him for a while, but as the helicopter drew steadily closer to the border, he became conscious of how tightly he was gripping his gun and how much sweat had already soaked into his combat jacket.

Among the men in the underground control room at Dimona, tension was also rising. Every picture on the bank of radar screens was the same – seven fluorescent dots approaching the evacuated zone, and two larger dots which were the echoes being received from the Galaxies.

The Galaxies were already leaving the eastern sector, their payloads of chalk hanging above the desert like drifting mist, waiting in the moonlight to join with the cargo from the AT 302s.

On the screens, shortly after 22.00 hours, the first dot entered the zone.

Pilotless, flying at an altitude of 2,000 feet under fully automatic control, the duster squadron responded to the Dimona radar. Each plane adjusted course, using the radar signals to correct their bearing and calculate the remaining distance to their target.

Like bees attracted to the domed hive of the reactor, the AT 302s moved into a dispersal pattern, flying alongside each other now, waiting for the electronic command to open their bays and begin discharging dust.

From hardened bunkers, twelve miles inside the evacuated zone, a wall of anti-aircraft fire rose up to meet them. At the same time, Chapperelle missiles streaked from their launchers, climbing into the night at the head of burning rocket trails.

In the night sky to the east of Dimona there was a flash of detonating warheads, bursts of concentrated light and the sound of distant thunder. The noise was followed by an eerie silence.

On the radar, the dots had gone. But the fog of reflections across the screens showed how far the dust had spread already.

The cloud descended slowly in the breeze, mixing with tendrils of chalk, becoming less concentrated as it thinned.

For nearly a minute it continued drifting harmlessly in the air. Then, in a blaze of glorious incandescence a false dawn broke across the Negev Desert, and from the pure white sun which was the fireball came a stentorian roar of fury.

In the control room, men waited for the shock wave. But the cloud had been too far away, and at ground level in the compound, the blast had been too weak to do anything more than make the palm trees shiver. Twelve miles away, where the explosion had carved out a 2,000-foot diameter crater in the sand, isolated pockets of dust continued to detonate or burn, but at the Dimona Nuclear Centre the emergency was over.

Further east, close to Israel's border with Jordan, the flash had illuminated the desert from the salt flats in the north to the Arava rift valley in the southern Negev, and for an instant, Redman had been able to see how low the Sea Knight had been flying. It was hugging the ground, following barren watercourses between brown and yellow mountains, skimming over the surface to avoid detection by Jordanian radar.

Fifteen seconds after the flash, information about the explosion had come in by radio, Kershner informing Redman personally to say that damage to the Centre was being assessed but that it was already thought to be minimal.

Since then, because the brigadier had been consulting with the navigator, Redman had received no further news either about Dimona or on their estimated time of arrival.

Kershner emerged from the cockpit now, stopping briefly to speak.

'We'll be landing in a couple of minutes,' he said. 'Khatib's on the move. We're going to be put down on the road east of Qasr et Tilha so we can be ready. Now, listen, I don't want you pretending you're an IDF regular. Your job's to identify Khatib. Dig yourself a hole somewhere and keep your eyes open. If you get into trouble, shoot low, from the waist down. Have you got that?'

Redman nodded. His mouth was dry.

'OK.' Kershner smiled. 'Good luck.'

The Sea Knight landed badly, rattling Redman's teeth and nearly making him drop his gun. He waited for the sergeant to open the hatch, then joined the line of men filing out into the sandstorm from the Sea Knight's rotors.

The helicopter was on the ground for less than half a minute before it took off again, this time flying north at low altitude to disappear into the darkness.

Standing by himself in the moonlight, Redman wondered whether Kershner intended to use the helicopter to strafe the convoy with machine-gun fire or whether that would defeat the object of trying to capture Khatib alive. But, judging by the activity of Kershner's men, this was going to be a ground operation, he decided, a straightforward ambush on the east flank of the convoy.

Soldiers were laying mines and running ribbons of plastic explosive across the road, working quickly, scattering sand behind them while other men were already digging trenches and erecting machine-guns on their tripods.

He walked off the road towards a depression in the sand, trying to guess how deep his foxhole needed to be and how long he had before the convoy arrived. He was still digging when a soldier came up to him to say the first truck was expected shortly.

Redman pulled back the slide on the SIG and let it go, hearing the metallic thunk of the first round being chambered. He placed the rifle on the ground in front of him then lay down in the shallow trench to wait.

Despite the breeze from the west, he heard the engines early. It reminded him of the peninsula again, of another engine, of another wait and of the foxhole he had shared with Debbie. Where was she now? he wondered. And what the hell were either of them doing here?

Moving fast, the convoy was travelling without headlights in the centre of the road. It drew closer, filling the night with noise.

The leading truck was nearly level with him when, as if in slow motion, Redman saw its front wheels blow off. They flew towards him, bouncing across the sand in front of his trench. A moment afterwards there was a flash from the plastic ribbons.

The convoy came to a standstill, one truck crashing into another ahead of it and overturning to block the road. Simultaneously, Kershner's men opened fire.

At such close range the noise was deafening. Mixed with the hammering of machine-guns and the blast from exploding mines there was the crack of grenades and a great deal of confused shouting. The confusion was made worse by trucks pulling off the road in an endeavour to escape, only to become bogged down in the sand. Revving engines added to the noise until the Sayerat Golani moved in to undertake the messier business of silencing the drivers while they searched through the convoy for the Syrian, Nassim Khatib.

From the safety of his trench Redman watched three or four trucks start to burn. Outclassed and outgunned, Khatib's men had stood no chance. For the few who dared to fight, the end came quickly, either by having their legs cut from under them by machine-gun fire or by Kershner's uncompromising policy of execution if he was certain they were not the man he was seeking.

200 yards away, flames from a burning gasoline tanker were throwing a glow over the desert, allowing Redman

to see that what little resistance there had been was all but over.

He stood up carrying his rifle, and began walking towards the flames. Here and there he encountered Kershner's men who were mopping up, searching each vehicle and using night-vision equipment to scan the shadows before they moved further on down the road. Redman went with them, half looking for Khatib but more anxious to discover if Debbie was all right.

He came across her at the tail end of the convoy where Kershner was covering her with an AK 47 while she approached a pair of military Land-Rovers. After checking the first one she skirted round behind it, being careful not to block Kershner's line of fire as she crept, gun in hand, towards the second.

She pulled on the door handle cautiously. But not cautiously enough.

No sooner had the door begun to open than Khatib had her by the throat.

It happened too swiftly for Redman to think of moving. Helplessly he watched Khatib get out using Debbie as a shield, twisting her arm behind her back to make her release her automatic.

Kershner, too, had been caught flat-footed. He raised the Kalashnikov, levelling the muzzle at Debbie's stomach.

Khatib was having trouble controlling Debbie until he stopped her struggles by ramming his gun into her neck. 'Will you sacrifice Miss Sarid in order to kill me?' he said to Kershner. 'What purpose will that serve now?'

Two Israeli soldiers stepped forwards. So did Redman.

'Ah, Mr Redman,' Khatib said. 'Perhaps I should have directed my question to you.'

'It's over,' Redman said. 'You don't understand. The dusters didn't get through.'

The Arab smiled. 'I regret it is you who misunderstand.' He bent down to pick up Debbie's automatic. 'Miss Sarid will be accompanying me in the Land-Rover. Should there be any attempt to stop us, I shall, of course, kill her.'

Debbie started to kick again. She fought wildly making it impossible for Khatib to hold her. Quickly he increased the pressure on her arm.

From twenty feet away, Redman heard the bone crack. Debbie screamed once, then became still, offering no further resistance while Khatib dragged her bodily into the Land-Rover behind him.

Kershner nodded to his men. At the same time he started to speak into his radio.

'No,' Redman yelled. 'Damn you Kershner. Tell your men to wait.' He saw the Land-Rover take to the sand, wheels spinning, already gathering speed.

'I'm sorry, Steven.' Kershner's face was grim. 'I can't let him get away. Debbie knows I can't.'

'I'll do it.' Redman steadied the SIG. 'You make your men hold their fire.'

In his sights, the Land-Rover was tiny, a disappearing target illuminated only in the flames of the burning convoy.

Centering the bead of his front sight on the cab, Redman thought despairingly of Owen, of Jennifer running like a rabbit along the airstrip, and of another girl he knew he could not save.

But as his finger tightened on the trigger, suddenly his mind broke free.

He neither heard the shot nor felt the recoil. Even after the Land-Rover rolled on to its side he was barely conscious of what he had done.

'God in heaven,' Kershner said quietly. 'Steven, look.'

Debbie was crawling out through the smashed windshield. Clutching her broken arm, she rose to her feet, stumbled, then began walking unsteadily back towards the road.

All along the convoy, men began sprinting across to help her. Like Kershner, Redman stayed where he was, still holding the SIG to his shoulder because he couldn't let it go.

He saw the men pick Debbie up and heard them calling out to Kershner.

The brigadier took Redman's gun from him. 'I don't know how the hell you did that,' he said.

'Nor do I.' Now it was over, Redman was drained of emotion altogether.

There were more shouts from the soldiers. Debbie was calling too, on her feet again, waving with her good arm.

Redman went with Kershner to meet her. She was going into shock and bleeding from a deep cut above her eye.

'It was Steven.' Kershner put his arm round her. 'A hundred and fifty yards in the dark.'

'Oh.' She winced in pain. 'There isn't time – we've got everything wrong. Khatib was laughing about it – a second before he was hit. The AT 302s were decoys. So was the squid boat. The real attack's coming from somewhere else.'

Sailing at four-and-a-half knots towards the Israeli coast on a dead flat sea, the mother-ship was matching its speed and direction to that of the wind. The westerly was constant, a breath of warm night air sweeping over the Mediterranean before it encountered the hotter surface of the Negev.

And riding on the wind, rising like gigantic bubbles one after another, cluster after cluster from the deck of the mother-ship were the balloons. They drifted upwards into the darkness, truck-sized envelopes of helium gas carrying their dust dispersal pods beneath them on the journey to their inland target sixty miles away.

Working in groups, the crew of the mother-ship was close to exhaustion. Only once before, for the second Pacific airburst experiment, had they inflated and launched balloons at such a rate. But then, because it had been no more than a test, the number of launches had been restricted, and the period over which the balloons had been released, much shorter. Tonight, for the attack on Dimona, the crew had been labouring for over four hours.

On the deck now stood the last few dispersal pods. As black as the kevlar fabric of the balloons which carried them, the pods too were made of plastic, sleek, glass-fibre containers already filled with their lethal mix of high explosive dust.

A shout came from the bow crew where one of the cables of a pod-support harness had snagged on a winch. For a moment there was danger of another balloon collapsing as two others had done when the wind had freshened. But no sooner were men preparing to cut the cable than the balloon steadied and began to rise again, pulling its pod smoothly from its cradle. Gaining height, nudging against a sister balloon which had been released at the same time from the stern, it disappeared into the night, drifting out over the sea towards Khan Yunis on the Gaza Strip.

Soon, travelling in thinner air, the balloons would inflate more fully to better catch the wind which would bear them eastwards over the Israeli coast. And there, once above the land, because their payload was too dangerous to destroy, they would be safe.

For another fifteen minutes the launching crews remained at their stations, too preoccupied with their jobs and with their arrangements to abandon ship before its hold was flooded, to wonder how quickly the balloons would be detected.

Like the AT 302s, the *Zhongshan* and the man who had so carefully planned the destruction of the Dimona complex, the end of the mother-ship was not long coming. At 23.00 hours, soon after it had been picked up by Israeli radar, but before the pilot of the F16 could make his rendezvous, it sank without trace into the shallow coastal waters of the sea.

* * *

Viewed from the intersection of Highway 86 and the road to Yeroham ten miles west of Dimona, the silent dark armada of balloons appeared to be off course.

'Now we know, don't we?' Kershner said. He leaned back against the car and lit a cigarette. 'It was the damn mother-ship all the time – Khatib's private weapon-launcher. No wonder it was never seen off Malaita, it was out at sea releasing balloons. And all we thought about was flight refuelling for the AT 302s. How the hell could we have ever been so stupid?'

Redman didn't answer. He was looking through binoculars at two of the leading balloons which were tangled together. They were too far south, he thought. But not quite far enough.

'Well?' Kershner asked. 'Are they heading straight for Dimona?'

'I can't tell. Depends if the wind changes again.'

'Crazy, isn't it?' Kershner blew out a stream of smoke. 'We thought the AT 302s were low technology, but at least we got a radar echo off them. Now, here we are using binoculars waiting to see what the wind's going to do. We might as well do a rain dance.'

Redman knew how worried Kershner was. For twelve hours the brigadier had been wrestling with the problem, blaming himself for not detecting the balloons earlier.

'Damn it,' Kershner said. 'There has to be a way. There has to be. I don't buy this crap about it being impossible to defend against a low-technology attack.'

'History,' Redman said. 'It's happened before. Five hundred years ago some people thought crossbows were the ultimate high-tech weapon system. The Europeans didn't have to train their armies to use crossbows. Anybody could shoot one. But the English stuck with the old-fashioned longbow.'

'And?' Kershner said.

'Low tech won. In those days, crossbows were useless in the rain because their strings stretched. Then the Europeans discovered English archers could shoot arrows twice as fast as a crossbowman. Low tech works. It isn't an illusion.'

Kershner's mood remained unchanged. 'Forty-eight tons of explosive dust is a hell of an illusion,' he said.

'If it hadn't been for the couple of balloons the coastguard found floating out at sea we'd be facing fifty tons,' Redman said.

'What's the difference?' Kershner took the binoculars steadying them on the roof of the car. 'The pods must have a timer in them or something. The leading balloons are losing height.'

'It's probably more clever than that,' Redman said. 'My guess is they're detecting radio or radar signals from Dimona. They might even be triangulating their target from commercial radio or TV channels. That's what's telling them to vent helium.'

'I can't believe we're watching this.' Kershner grunted. 'Why the hell we never shot them down before they hit land, I'll never know.'

'You didn't know they were in the air until the sun came up. It's no good worrying about what you should've done. I've told you – Khatib's been real smart; black balloons at night; fabric, glass fibre and plastic harnesses that don't show up on radar and the clever bit – forty-eight warheads you can't get rid of without triggering the whole lot. The system's damn near foolproof. Owen would have loved it.'

'Yes.' Kershner threw away his cigarette. 'We'd better get back to the centre. I have to decide if I want the Americans to try the chalk again.'

'It didn't work before,' Redman said. 'There's only one way to handle this, the same way as last night. Wait until the balloons are inside the evacuated zone then hit them with everything you've got.' He climbed into the car. 'Sure it's going to be nasty, but it's going to be ten miles away from the reactor.'

'Can you imagine what it would be like if we hadn't evacuated – if I'd had to choose between the Nuclear Centre or somewhere like Beersheba? A hundred-thousand people right in line.'

'You don't have to choose,' Redman said. 'You've got an empty western sector.'

'Ten miles,' Kershner muttered. 'Sixteen or seventeen kilometres for forty-eight tons of enhanced dust. Jesus.'

He drove slowly back along the highway to Dimona, not speaking again until he parked the car outside the security building.

'Did you phone the hospital?' he asked.

Redman nodded. 'This morning. She's fine; wanted to come out here and watch.'

'Did she tell you that was a head shot on Khatib?'

'I was aiming for the tyres.' Redman didn't want to discuss it. 'Is it OK if I wait in the control room?'

'Sure.' Kershner glanced at his watch. 'Three-and-a-bit hours,' he said. 'If you have any good ideas before then, get hold of me on the telephone.'

In the underground control room, time was crawling. This afternoon, instead of radar screens there were television monitors, three of them showing the Dimona compound and reactor dome, the remainder displaying pictures of approaching balloons at different magnifications.

Some of the close-up shots showed that more than two of the pods had become tangled during their flight across the desert. Although there were clusters of balloons, just as there were rogues which had drifted away by themselves, the majority could be contained in a circle that Redman guessed would be less than two miles across – a tight enough pack to spread an even cloud of dust, he thought. Maybe one that would be the airborne equivalent of a valley-full if Kershner was unlucky.

He stood alone at the back of the room, watching the minutes tick over on the digital clock above the monitors, wondering what would happen if the reactor or the cooling tank were unable to withstand the shock wave.

At 1.19 in the afternoon the first balloon crossed into the evacuated zone. By two o'clock, twenty-three more balloons had followed. They were much lower now, with sunlight glinting off the polished surface of their pods.

Redman watched them draw closer on the screens, counting how many were inside the zone and estimating how close the leading balloon would be to the reactor by the time the last one had safely crossed the line.

The ground-control officer was counting too, second by second, minute by minute, sliding a thin plastic disc across his map. The disc was all he had, a transparent circle defining the limits of the anticipated over-pressure from the blast.

When the rim of the disc touched the outmost building in the compound he gave the command to fire.

Today the anti-aircraft guns were silent. Instead, from dozens of points within the sector, optically-guided missiles soared into the sky. They left streaks behind them on the TV screens, arrows of light, each one leading to an individual dust-filled pod.

Redman watched in fascination as over a hundred warheads came to life. He saw dust spreading out from the debris, saw more missiles climbing through the dust cloud, and then, an instant before the screens went white he saw the first red bolts of lightning strike.

Ninety feet below the ground, the blast was not unlike a series of jolts from a small earthquake, a gentle rocking of the room. A coffee cup fell off a table somewhere and the lights flickered, but the shaking was over almost as soon as it had begun.

Men were busier now, anxious to discover how serious the blast had been on the surface, checking through the systems in each machon one after another from level one to level eight where the most radioactive elements were processed. At the same time other men attended to an array of instruments and lights to determine the extent of the damage to the reactor building and the cooling tank. But long before the monitors came back on line, in the control room, anxiety had given way to jubilation.

Showing on some of the screens now was what appeared to be a dirty thundercloud across the sun. Other monitors displayed different pictures – pictures of an unharmed compound in which every building had survived. The palm trees along the eastern perimeter fence appeared to have suffered most, but at least half a dozen remained standing, and except for some upturned cars, there was little obvious evidence of how severe the blast had been.

Redman left the room, taking the elevator to the surface where he made his way up on to the catwalk to join a handful of other people. They were staring at the distant crater and the approaching cloud, stunned by the sight of four square miles of sky filled with swirling sand, smoke and unburned dust.

Although the scene was undeniably spectacular, for Redman it was an anticlimax. Unlike the experiment in the valley, this explosion had been free to expand out over the desert and, as a result, apart from the crater and the thundercloud, there was not a great deal more to see. There was no burning forest, fleeing wildlife or smouldering piles of debris. And, despite the metallic taste in his mouth, for the moment at least, the air above the compound was reasonably clear.

He stayed at the catwalk for a few more minutes, realizing now that for him the fifth and final explosion had been more than an anticlimax. Instead of relief or elation he felt dull, and instead of wanting to find Kershner to offer his congratulations, his thoughts were centred on tomorrow – on the plan for the future that depended not on Kershner, but on someone else altogether.

*   *   *

In the street below the balcony, the residents of Givat
Alijah were coming home – schoolchildren, teenagers on
bicycles and adults – all hurrying along in the late
afternoon sunshine as though they thought the day might
suddenly end before they reached wherever they were
going.

Redman wondered how many of them appreciated
what had really happened at Dimona. Even after
saturation media coverage, the people seemed uncon-
cerned, apparently refusing to believe the defence network of their country had all but failed them.

And yet in the end, the superbomb too had failed,
Redman thought. It was an aberration – but a weapon the
survivors of Hiroshima would understand even if the
good citizens of Tel Aviv did not.

'Help.' Debbie came from the kitchen balancing a row
of wobbling beer cans on her plaster cast.

Two of the cans toppled off before she could reach the
table.

Kershner picked them up. 'You and Steven will have to
finish these,' he said. 'I've been here too long already.
You're supposed to be resting that arm, not using it to
serve drinks.'

She laughed. 'I have to use it for something.'

'Take care of it,' Kershner said. 'That's an order. Now I
really must go.' He turned to shake hands with Redman.
'Steven, are you sure you don't want to stay a few more
days?'

'I'm sure. I need to get on with a few things.'

'Like sinking Corliss? Or are you going straight back to
Airtech?'

Redman shook his head. 'Neither. I don't think Corliss
needs any help to sink. And after all this, I'd rather join
the IDF than go on working for Airtech. Hawthorne
wouldn't have me, anyway.' He accompanied the

brigadier to the door.

'You know you're welcome in Israel anytime, don't you?' Kershner paused with his hand on the door. 'On your own terms.'

'Yeah, I know.' Redman felt awkward about saying goodbye.

'OK. If this doesn't sound too trite, I'd like to say I'm glad we met each other.' Kershner let himself out, closing the door quietly behind him.

Debbie was sitting on the balcony rail when Redman returned. She didn't look round until he spoke to her.

'So what happens now?' he said.

'Kershner's sending me to Paris, but I'm calling in to see my brother-in-law on the way – you know, Geoff Hinton in Seattle. He's invited me to stay with him. I'm not sure how long I'll be there. Until my cast comes off, I suppose.'

'That night in Owen's apartment.' He hesitated. 'You said you'd go anywhere with me, do anything I asked you to do.'

She left the rail and came to stand in front of him. 'Is that what you want?'

'I was going to tell you before – when we were at the Church of St Peter. I didn't know how to explain then and I don't know how to say it now. All I know is I can't think straight when you're anywhere near me and I can't think at all when you're not.' He paused. 'You can't go to Paris. You have to come with me.'

She met his eyes. 'You thought I slept with you to get information for the IDF. You told me – over and over and over. You said you didn't trust me, that you never would.'

It was going wrong. Because of his clumsiness, she was slipping from his grasp. But when he searched for more words to explain, he found there were none.

'Are you in love with me?'

He nodded.

'It won't work,' she said softly. 'Maybe once it would have. I don't know – neither of us knows.' She stood on tiptoe to kiss him on the mouth. 'But I won't ever forget you, Steven Redman. You're a very wonderful person.'

From some distant point in his mind, Redman's future came crashing down around him. Her eyes were still upon him and the half smile was on her lips again, but she was gone – gone from his life to become another memory, an unfulfilled dream of all the tomorrows he had thrown away.

Twelve

Even in the light of late evening the atolls were the same. So were the islands, all of them floating like green pin-cushions in the same sapphire sea as though they had been waiting for his return.

The Air Niugini flight attendant came to see if she could help.

'Those are the Russells, aren't they?' Redman pointed. 'Just down there behind the wing.'

'That's right.' She smiled. 'Have you been to the Solomons before? You don't look like a business man, if you don't mind me saying so.'

'I was here a while ago. But I'm not sure if I'm on a business trip this time.'

'Well, have a nice stay anyway,' she said. 'We'll be on the ground in a few minutes.'

When she'd gone, he looked back out of the window watching the shadows spreading out over the sea until the pilot turned south to begin his approach to Henderson airport.

Full circle, Redman thought. From one side of the damn world to the other and back again, a journey without purpose, or almost without purpose. It was hard to believe it had been May when he was here last, and harder still to reconcile the disappearance of an Airtech Eagle with everything that had happened since that day two months ago when he'd first stepped off the plane in the Solomons.

He passed through customs and immigration, deliberately thinking more of Jennifer Decker than of Debbie, endeavouring to concentrate his attention on being back in Honiara instead of wondering about Tel Aviv or Paris or wherever Debbie was by now.

Jimmy was waiting for him outside the terminal building.

'Hi.' Redman shook hands with the smiling islander. 'You got my message, then.'

'At the resort there is a fax for me. And before that, maybe two or three weeks ago, there is a phone call from someone who says he is a friend of yours.'

'Kershner,' Redman said.

Jimmy nodded. 'So first I know you are OK, then I understand you are coming back to Honiara.'

'That's not a problem, is it?'

'No. It is all fixed by someone before I go to the police with the photographs. I am pleased you are here.'

'So am I. Did you get a car for me?'

'I rent one.' Jimmy grinned. 'So we can together find a good boat, a better one than the *Kwaibala*, eh?' He carried Redman's case over to a white Subaru station wagon. 'I book you a nice room for tonight at the Mendana, but tomorrow you will please come to stay with me and my wife Louise. She has told me I must ask you.'

'I'll see.' Redman got into the car. If he was going to buy a boat at all, he had no intention of rushing things, and in the circumstances, he thought it might be better to spend a few days by himself in Honiara before accepting the invitation to stay at Jimmy's home.

'Outside the car-park you must turn left,' Jimmy said. 'Maybe you forget.'

'I remember.' Redman wound down the window, enjoying the warmth and moisture of the air on his skin. 'I remember every damn minute.'

'You find the men who kill Mrs Decker? The white men who make the silver water on Malaita?'

'Yeah,' Redman said. 'I found them. I'll tell you about it when we've got some cold beers lined up. It's a long story.'

'You tell me tomorrow. This evening I visit my uncle in Visale. He is to give me the names of men who wish to sell boats.'

'OK.' Redman stretched. 'I'm pretty tired, anyway. I came a long way round to tie up some loose ends in the States. It feels like I've been on the move for a week.'

'But you will stay in the Islands now?'

'Yeah, I think so. I wasn't sure this was a good idea, but now I'm here, I don't care whether it is or not. I'll make it a good idea.'

He turned the car on to Mendana Avenue, slowing down as the traffic became heavier and as more and more Solomon Islanders started spilling out of shops and restaurants along the waterfront. Like the view from the aircraft, the atmosphere in Honiara was exactly as Redman remembered it, a relaxed busyness that seemed to be unique to the Solomon Islands.

He parked the Subaru outside the hotel, leaving the motor running while he collected his case from the rear seat.

'You take the car,' he said. 'I don't need it tonight.'

Jimmy slipped behind the wheel. 'I pick you up in the morning, yes?'

'Sure. But there's no hurry. I need to slow down. That's why I'm here.'

'You slow down tonight, I think.' Jimmy's face split into another grin. 'Go to bed early.' He drove away with his arm waving out the window.

Redman walked into the cool of the hotel lobby and

checked in, leaving his case at the desk while he went to buy a bottle of bourbon from the bar. When he came back the porter was waiting.

'It's OK, thanks.' Redman carried the case upstairs himself. As well as feeling washed out he was conscious of having reached the end point of his journey before he was ready for it. The feeling became worse once he was inside his room. So this was it, he thought. The best he could do. Another hotel room, another bottle and another fresh start.

To make sure it truly was a fresh start he went over to the window and stared out towards Point Cruz and the blue water of Iron Bottom Sound where fishing boats were berthing for the night. The scene was suitably unreal, a hundred-year-old painting of somewhere so far removed from the world of Kershner, Corliss and a girl called Debbie that he might as well have been on another planet.

He left the window, intending to unpack before he poured himself a drink, but stopped when he was no more than half-way across the room.

In the centre of the coffee table, standing by itself was a *nguzunguzu*.

Redman picked it up and rubbed his fingers over the polished wood. There was a fragrance to it, the sweet scent of oil, of perfume and of Debbie's freshly-washed blonde hair.

Before he turned round he knew she was there.

'I changed my mind.' She stood in the doorway to the bedroom, speaking so quietly he could barely hear her.

'Why?'

'I couldn't let go of you. After you'd gone, I knew I couldn't. I talked to Kershner, he said he thought you were heading for the Solomons so I phoned Jimmy.' She faltered. 'It's all right, isn't it?'

'Come here,' Redman said. 'Just come here.'

She came to him, standing absolutely still while he untied the ribbon from her hair.

'Don't move,' he said.

'Why?'

'In case it isn't really you.'

'Oh. Aren't you going to kiss me? It's only my arm that's in plaster. I won't break or anything.'

He ran his fingers through her hair, studying her face, not trusting himself to speak.

'It isn't dark yet,' she said softly. 'Or doesn't that matter anymore?'

'Nothing matters anymore.' He smiled at her. Then he picked her up and carried her slowly to the bedroom.

Outside, the streets along the waterfront were quieter now, bathed in a final glow of sunlight, cooled by an ocean breeze. Already the island was being lulled to sleep on another warm Pacific night. But long before the light had faded and the breeze had died away, for two people lost to everything except each other, this would become not just another night, but one bearing the promise of endless summer nights in which the events that had brought them here would slowly but surely be forgotten.